IN THE MISO SOUP

BY THE SAME AUTHOR

Almost Transparent Blue
69
Coin Locker Babies

IN THE MISO SOUP

Ryu Murakami

Translated by Ralph McCarthy

BLOOMSBURY

First published in Great Britain 2005

Bloomsbury Publishing Plc, 38 Soho Square, London W1D 3HB

A CIP catalogue record for this book is available from the British Library

ISBN 0 7475 7405 7

10 9 8 7 6 5 4 3 2 1

Printed in Great Britain by Clays Ltd, St Ives plc

All papers used by Bloomsbury Publishing are natural, recyclable products
made from wood grown in well-managed forests. The manufacturing processes
conform to the environmental regulations of the country of origin

IN THE MISO SOUP

1

My name is Kenji.

As I pronounced these words in English I wondered why we have so many ways of saying the same thing in Japanese. Hard-boiled: *Ore no na wa Kenji da.* Polite: *Watashi wa Kenji to moshimasu.* Casual: *Boku wa Kenji.* Gay: *Atashi Kenji 'te iu no yo!*

"Oh, so you're Kenji!" The overweight American tourist made a big show of being delighted to see me. "Nice to meet you," I said and shook his hand. This was near Seibu Shinjuku Station, at a hotel that might rate about two-and-a-half stars overseas. A moment I won't forget—the first time I ever met Frank.

I had just turned twenty, and though my English is far from perfect I was working as a "nightlife guide" for foreign tourists. Basically I specialize in what you might call sex tours, so it's not as if my English needs to be flawless. Since AIDS, the sex industry hasn't exactly welcomed foreigners with open arms—in fact, most of the clubs are pretty blatant about refusing service to *gaijin*—but lots of visitors from overseas are still determined to play, and they're the ones who pay me to guide them to relatively safe cabarets and massage parlors and S&M bars and "soaplands" and what have you. I'm not employed by a company and don't even have an office, but by running a simple ad in an English-language tourist magazine I make enough to rent a nice studio apartment in Meguro, take my girl out for Korean barbecue once in a while, and listen to the music I like and read the things I want to read. I should mention, though, that my mother, who runs a little clothes shop in

Shizuoka Prefecture, thinks I'm enrolled in a college preparation course. Mom brought me up on her own after Dad died when I was fourteen. I had friends back in high school who thought nothing of slapping their own mothers around, but you'd never catch me hurting mine. Much as I hate to disappoint Mom, though, I have no plans to go to college. I definitely don't have the background in science and math to go for a professional degree, and all a degree in "the arts" would get me is a cubicle in an office somewhere. My dream, not that I've ever had much hope of realizing it, is to save up a fair amount of money and go to America.

"Is this Kenji Tours? My name's Frank, I'm a tourist from the United States of America?"

When the phone rang, late in the morning of December 29 last year, I was reading a newspaper article about this high-school girl who'd been murdered. According to the article, her corpse had been dumped at a trash collection site in a relatively untraveled alley in the Kabuki-cho district of Shinjuku with her arms, legs, and head cut off. The victim had been one of a group of high-school girls who openly peddled sex in the area and was well known at nearby "love hotels." No eyewitnesses had come forward, and investigators had no solid leads as yet. The article went on to editorialize that one's heart went out to the victim, of course, but perhaps this incident would help instill in today's teens a proper understanding of the potential horror behind those fashionable words "compensated dating," and that all the girls in the victim's group had now sworn off what they flippantly refer to as "selling it."

"Hi, Frank." I tossed the newspaper on the table and gave him my standard greeting. "How you doing?"

"I'm all right. I saw your ad in this magazine and wondered if I can hire you to show me around."

"*Tokyo Pink Guide*?"

"How'd you guess?"

"It's the only magazine we advertise in."

"Aha! So can I hire you for three nights, starting tonight?"

"Are you alone, Frank, or with a group?"

"It's just me. Is that a problem?"

"No, but for one person it's kind of expensive—¥10,000 from six to nine; ¥20,000 from nine to midnight; and ¥10,000 for each hour after midnight. I don't charge tax, but you pay all expenses, including any meals and drinks we have together."

"That's fine. I'd like the nine to midnight course, starting tonight—if I can book you for three nights."

Three nights took us through New Year's Eve, and there was just one problem. I have this girlfriend named Jun—a high-school girl who, by the way, is dead set against "selling it"—and I'd broken my promise to spend Christmas with her. She didn't like that one bit, and just the other day I'd given my solemn word, locking pinkies with her and everything, that we would absolutely be together for the countdown on New Year's Eve. Jun can be kind of hard to deal with when she gets mad, but I wanted the job. After almost two years of doing this sort of work I hadn't saved nearly as much money as I'd hoped to. I told Frank okay and told myself that on New Year's Eve I'd just invent some excuse and cut out early.

"I'll be at your hotel at ten of nine," I said.

Frank was waiting for me in the cafeteria off the lobby, drinking a beer. He'd described himself as white and stocky and looking a bit like Ed Harris in profile, and said he'd be wearing a necktie with a pattern of white swans, but he was the only foreigner in the place anyway. I introduced myself and shook his hand, studying his face and not finding the least resemblance to Ed Harris from any angle.

"Shall we get started right away?" he said.

"Up to you, Frank. But if you have any questions, now might be a good time. The magazines don't tell you everything you need to know about nightlife in Tokyo."

"Oh, I like the sound of that."

"What?"

"'Nightlife in Tokyo'—just the sound of those words is kind of exciting, isn't it?"

Frank certainly didn't remind me of the soldiers or astronauts or whatever that Ed Harris portrays—he looked more like a stockbroker or something. Not that I have any idea what an actual stockbroker is supposed to look like. I just mean he struck me as sort of drab and nondescript.

"How old are you, Kenji?"

"Twenty."

"Oh? Well, they say the Japanese look young for their age, but that's exactly what I would have guessed."

I had bought two suits at a discount clothing outlet in the suburbs and always wore one or the other when I was working. In winter, like now, I needed an overcoat and muffler too. My hair is average length, and I don't bleach it or have any piercings or anything. Most sex clubs are wary of people whose appearance is eccentric in any way.

"And you, Frank?"

"I'm thirty-five."

He smiled as he said it, and that's when I first noticed this thing about his face. It was a very average sort of face, but you couldn't have judged his age from it. Depending on the angle of the light, one moment he looked like he could be in his twenties, and the next in his forties or even fifties. I'd worked for nearly two hundred foreigners by now, most of them Americans, but I'd never seen a face quite like this one. It took me a while to pinpoint exactly what was so odd about it. The skin. It looked almost artificial, as if he'd been horribly burned and the doctors had resurfaced his face with this fairly realistic man-made material. For some reason these thoughts stirred up the unpleasant memory of that newspaper article, the murdered schoolgirl. I sipped my coffee.

"When did you arrive in Japan?"

The day before yesterday, Frank said. He was drinking his beer at a ridiculously slow pace. He'd raise the glass to his lips and sort of peer at the foam awhile, like someone contemplating a cup of hot tea, then take a tiny sip and swallow as if forcing down some foul-tasting medicine. This guy could turn out to be a tremendous tightwad, I thought, remembering the passage in a Tokyo guidebook a lot of my American clients used. *Never eat meals at hotel restaurants. Fast-food joints are everywhere, and you can always just grab a burger nearby. If you have to meet someone in the hotel restaurant or bar, feel free to linger for an hour or two over a single beer. Coffee is shockingly expensive and therefore to be avoided, but those who want first-hand experience of the nose-bleed prices at Tokyo's top hotels are advised to order a fresh orange juice. Extracted from the grandiose glass cooler where it's kept, this overgrown thimbleful of the juice and pulp of a mere orange will set you back at least eight and often as much as fifteen dollars. Enjoy the taste of the Japanese government's tariff system!*

"You're here on business?"

"That's right."

"Everything going well?"

"I'll say it is! I import Toyota radiators from Southeast Asia, and I came here to finalize the licensing agreement? But since we've already been sending drafts back and forth by e-mail we managed to wrap it all up in one day, so what can I say? It went perfectly!"

This didn't sound right to me. Here in Japan, most businesses were having their last workday today, the twenty-ninth, but Americans would have been on holiday since before Christmas. And nothing about this hotel or Frank's clothes matched all that stuff about Toyota and licensing agreements and e-mail. From my experience so far, the legitimate businessmen who visit Shinjuku tend to stay in the top four hotels—the Park Hyatt, the Century Hyatt, the Hilton, and the Keio Plaza, in that order—and to take extra care with their wardrobe, especially if they're working on an important contract. Frank's suit looked even cheaper than my own Smart Young Businessman's Three-Piece at the Special Konaka Discount Price of ¥29,800 (Second Pair of Slacks Included). It was a tacky cream color and too small, to the extent that the crotch of his trousers seemed on the verge of splitting.

"That's great," I said. "Now, what is it you want tonight, basically?"

"Sex."

Frank said this with a bashful grin, but it wasn't like any bashful grin I'd ever seen on an American before.

Nobody, I don't care what country they're from, has a perfect personality. Everyone has a good side and a side that's not so good. That's something I learned working at this job. What's good about Americans, if I can generalize a little, is that they have a kind of openhearted innocence. And what's not so good is that they can't imagine any world outside the States, or any value system different from their own. The Japanese have a similar defect, but Americans are even worse about trying to force others to do whatever they themselves believe to be right. American clients often forbid me to smoke and sometimes even make me accompany them on their daily jogs. In a word, they're childish—but maybe that's what makes their smile so appealing. Robert de Niro, Kevin Costner, Brad Pitt—the winning, bashful grin of the American actor is like part of the national character. There was nothing appealing about Frank's grin, though. Unnerving, is more like it. The artificial-looking skin of his face twisted into a whorl of wrinkles, making him look almost disfigured.

"According to *Tokyo Pink Guide*, a man can find anything he wants here," he said.

"You mean the magazine?"

"The book, too."

Tokyo Pink Guide, the book, is by a man who calls himself Stephen Langhorne Clemens. It describes, in a pretty entertaining way, the various aspects of the sex industry in Tokyo—hostess bars, host bars, peep shows, strip clubs, massage parlors, call girls, and even the S&M and gay and lesbian scenes. The only problem is that the information is out of date. Sex businesses tend to sprout up and wither away in cycles of about three months. The magazine comes out twice a year, and even the information in that is soon outdated.

Of course, if the magazine covered everything, I might be out of a job. But you'll never see a weekly city guide like *Pia* or *Tokyo Walker* published in English. Not in this country. Japan is fundamentally uninterested in foreigners, which is why the knee-jerk response to any trouble is simply to shut them all out. Maybe I shouldn't complain because it's the main reason my services are needed, but ever since the advent of HIV—and even as the number of infected Japanese soars—most sex clubs have continued to ban all gaijin.

"I want to try a lot of things, go to a lot of different places." Frank showed me the bashful grin again, and I couldn't help looking away. "According to what I've read, you can find it all here—Tokyo's like a department store of sex!"

Frank took the *Tokyo Pink Guide* out of a dark-brown shoulder bag beside his chair and put it on the table. The magazine, not the book. It was only a few pages thick—more like a brochure, really—and the photo on the front was of crummy quality, as if to ensure that no one mistook it for anything they'd actually want to read. The publisher is a man in his fifties named Yokoyama who used to be in the news department of a TV station. Yokoyama-san has been incredibly nice to me. He refuses to charge me for my ad, for one thing, even though he doesn't seem to be making any money on his rag. He claims that the Japanese need to give people in other countries more information about themselves, and that sports and music and sex are the only types of information that have true international appeal, and that of those three the one that speaks most directly to people's common humanity is sex, and that the reason he keeps struggling to scrape the money together to publish the magazine is because he wants to make a difference, but I'm afraid he's basically just a guy who likes dirty stuff.

"This is a country," Frank said, "where you can take care of every conceivable sexual need, right? I definitely want to go to Kabuki-cho. I checked it out on the sex map while I was waiting for you, and it's right near here, isn't it? Look at all the marks for sex clubs in Kabuki-cho. It looks like the Andromeda galaxy!"

The magazine contains maps not only of Shinjuku but of Roppongi and

Shibuya and Kinshicho and Yoshiwara, and even the sleazy parts of Yokohama and Chiba and Kawasaki. But Frank was right, Kabuki-cho was the undisputed champion. Sex businesses are indicated with a mark like a pair of boobs, and from the Koma Theater to Kuyakusho Avenue the boobs crowded each other like grapes on the vine.

"Where should we go first, Kenji?"

"You want to try several different clubs, then?"

"Yes."

"You know you can get sex right away if you want," I said, lowering my voice. "You could even have a girl delivered to this hotel. Club-hopping in Kabuki-cho can be fun, but it can also be pretty expensive."

The cafeteria we were in wasn't very big, and Frank had a loud voice. The waiters and the other customers were shooting annoyed glances at us. Even people who don't understand much English tend to get the gist of this sort of talk.

"Oh, money's no problem," said Frank.

The New Year's holiday was nearly upon us, but Kabuki-cho was as busy as ever. A decade ago, the sex industry catered mainly to middle-aged men, but now there are lots of young customers, too. It seems that more and more young dudes can't be bothered to look for a girlfriend or a fuck-buddy. Overseas these guys would probably turn gay, but Japan has the Sex Industry.

As he blinked at Kabuki-cho's neon lights and the more flamboyant touts and barkers in their kitschy outfits and the women standing here and there on the street trying to catch his eye, Frank slapped me on the shoulder and said "This is great!" It was freezing out there, but he wasn't even wearing an overcoat. With his short, lumpy frame wrapped in that tacky suit, Frank was no treat for the eyes, but he blended right in with the streets and crowds of Kabuki-cho.

A group of black guys in matching red windbreakers were touting for a newly opened "show pub" that featured foreign dancers. They were handing out fliers and giving their pitch to the men walking by. "What you gentlemen need is to see some world-class nude dancing—at the unheard-of price of only ¥7000 for a full hour!" Their Japanese was flawless. Frank tried to take a flier and was ignored at first. He stood with his hand out, smiling, and the black guy reached around him to hand one to a passing Japanese. I don't think the guy meant anything in particular by it. He may have had a certain reaction to Frank being white, or it could be that his employers told him to give precedence to Japanese over impoverished-looking foreigners, but in any case he clearly wasn't trying to yank Frank's chain. Frank's expression underwent a disturbing change, though. It was only for a moment, but it startled me. The artificial-looking skin of his cheeks twitched and quivered, and his eyes lost any recognizable human quality, as if someone had turned out the light behind them. They might have been beads of smoked glass. The tout didn't notice. He handed Frank a flier and said something in English that I couldn't quite hear. I think it was simply about the dancers being not from the U.S. but Australia and South America, but the light came back on in Frank's eyes, and his face relaxed. Something ugly had reared its head for a second and then vanished again.

Frank looked at the flier and said to the guy: "Your Japanese is amazing, where are you from?" When the guy said New York, Frank beamed at him and told him the Knicks were on a winning streak and looking like a new team. I know that, the guy said, handing another passerby a flier.

"We get all the NBA action—hell, TV here even tells you where Michael Jordan played golf on his day off, and what his score was."

"You don't say," Frank said and slapped him on the back. As we walked away, Frank draped his arm over my shoulder and said: "What a terrific fellow, Kenji—a man in a million!" As if he'd known him for years.

We came to a stop in front of a sign with one big eye.

"Even I know what this is," Frank said. "A peep show, right?"

I explained how this one worked.

"You get in a booth with a one-way mirror and watch the girls undress. In each booth is a little semicircular hole, and if you put your dick in there they jerk you off. These places were really popular until just recently."

"They aren't popular now? How come?"

"Well, peep shows are cheap. To turn a profit they need a lot of customers, but they can't pay the girls that much. If the money isn't good all the young and pretty girls quit, and if the girls aren't young and pretty the customers stop coming. It's a vicious circle."

"How much is it? The sign says ¥3000—what's that, $25? Kenji, $25 for a peep show and a hand job? That *is* cheap!"

"That's just what it costs to get in. You have to tip another $20 or $30 for the hand job."

"Still, that's not bad. The girl who does the stripping is the one who jerks you off, right?"

"Usually you can't see who's on the other side of the wall. That's why there were rumors about old ladies doing it, or gay guys. Which is another reason these places aren't so popular anymore."

"So it's not worth going in?"

"Well, they *are* inexpensive, and you wouldn't need an interpreter. I could go get some coffee or something and you'd only have to pay for one."

As we talked, the touts began flocking around us. Most of them were from the newer "lingerie pubs" and none of them knew who I was. The old hands know me by sight, but of the maybe two hundred touts on this street at least eighty percent were rookies. The dudes who become touts are generally at the end of their rope: guys who for one reason or another can't work anywhere else, or who are desperate for some quick cash—which is why they tend to come and go so quickly and why they aren't necessarily reliable. You can generally trust the touts who've been around a long time, though.

"Kenji, what are these fellows saying?"

I took a moment to explain what a lingerie pub was, but the touts were talking much too fast for me to translate: "Absolutely no additional charges!

Normally it would be ¥9000 but because it's the end of the year and we've just opened we're only charging ¥5000! Would I lie to you? When I say the girls are young, I'm talking barely legal! Naturally your foreign friend is welcome too! It's just down those steps over there! Right this way! We have online karaoke and a full catalogue of English songs! Please, gentlemen! If you're not satisfied with the quality of the girls or the atmosphere of the pub, you're absolutely at liberty to turn around and walk out! You can't pass up an opportunity like this! Once the new year arrives, the price goes right back up! What have you got to lose?"

As we walked away from this fairly overbearing pack of touts, Frank said, "I heard that the Japanese were nice, but this is amazing." He kept turning to look back at them, still milling about in front of the peep show. Most of them were wearing cheap suits like mine. This was Kabuki-cho, not Roppongi, and you didn't see many designer clothes on these streets. The only way you could tell most of the customers from the touts was that the customers were walking and the touts looked like they were loitering. Even from a distance, touts have something lonesome about them. Most of the guys I know who've done the job a long time are sort of worn thin—not physically run down, but like something's eroded away inside. Even when you're talking to them face to face you have this feeling of not connecting, as if the words just pass right through them. Sometimes they remind me of the Invisible Man, but I've never quite understood why they end up that way.

"These fellows are nothing like the seedy characters who work for American sex clubs," said Frank. "They're more like Eagle Scouts or something! How do they find the energy to be so friendly all night?"

"For every customer they bring in they get a commission."

"Well, that's only fair, I guess. But can you trust what they tell you?"

"It's best to be suspicious if the price seems too cheap."

The idea of a lingerie pub clearly appealed to Frank.

"Shall we go see some Japanese girls in their underwear, then, for starters?" he said.

"You can't have sex there."

"I know. I want to build up to that slowly anyway, and right now girls in their underwear seems like the best way to start."

"One hour, at this time of night, will cost ¥7000 to ¥9000 per person, and since hardly any of the girls speak English you'll have to pay for me too. There are pubs where you can touch the girls and pubs where you can't, and there are ones that put on shows and ones where the girls will dance on your table, but the prices don't vary that much."

"I prefer your normal kind of place, where the girls just sit next to you and talk," Frank said. "After all, if the price doesn't go up much even with all those options, then the pubs without the options must have the prettiest girls. Right, Kenji?"

I found a tout I knew and had him guide us to his pub. Satoshi was the same age as me, twenty. At eighteen he'd come to Tokyo from Yamanashi—or Nagano, I forget which—to attend a college prep school, and almost immediately went mental. I didn't know him then, but he once showed me a souvenir of those times. He invited me to his apartment in the wee hours one morning and pulled out a set of children's building blocks. It seems he used to ride around and around on the Yamanote Line with them, building castles on the floor of the train. Why would you do that, I asked him, and he shrugged. I don't know, man, I found them at Kiddyland and I just wanted to buy them and play with them somewhere, you know, and then I thought the train would be good, and it *was* good, man, it's fun trying to build a castle on a moving train, you can like lose yourself or whatever and not have all these weird thoughts, because at the time I kept having this weird thought about poking some little girl's eyes with a pin or a toothpick or a hypodermic needle, something pointy like that, and it scared me to think about what if I really did it, but once I started playing with my blocks on the floor of the train I forgot about that obsession or compulsion or whatever you call it, because it's not easy to stack blocks on the floor of a moving train, you really need to concentrate, and the Yamanote Line has some major curves, like between Harajuku and Yoyogi especially, and I had to cradle the little castle in my arms to keep it from falling apart. Sure I got yelled at, man. I don't know how many times conductors and station workers yelled at me, and I was even picked up by the railway cops a few times, but, hell, it's not like I was doing it during rush hour. Anyway, this went on for about six months, but then when I came to Kabuki-cho it cured me. Hey, I wouldn't say I love Kabuki-cho—I mean, I doubt if anybody *loves* it—but it's an amazingly easy place to be, and who's going to think about sticking needles in little girls' eyes when they're working in a town they like and have a chance to go to the university of their choice?

"One of our girls speaks a little English, man. If she's available I'll send her over to you for no extra charge."

Satoshi led Frank and me to a green door in the basement of a nearby building. I'd been to this pub any number of times, but I can't remember what it was called. All these places have similar names, for one thing. No one racks their brains to come up with something original because no customer in Kabuki-cho would ever choose a club just because it has a clever name.

The interiors of all lingerie pubs look pretty much the same, too. They don't actually share a common design, just the same sort of crappy materials. Frank looked at the girls clustered on the sofas in their underwear and gave his bizarre bashful grin.

The girl who could speak a little English was called Reika. She wore her hair up and expensive-looking purple lace underwear, and aside from a flattish nose and coarse skin, she was pretty cute. Along with Reika came Rie, a big girl with average features and a physique like a volleyball player, who liked white underwear and laughed a lot. Just because a woman laughs a lot doesn't mean she's got a sunny disposition, though, especially in the sex trade. Once we were all seated and the whiskey tray was brought to the table, Satoshi turned to me and said thanks, man, and headed back out to the street. There were only two other customers in the place, and I vaguely wondered how much Satoshi would get for bringing us here. We know each other fairly well, but we don't talk about stuff like that. Not trying to find out too much about other people's finances is one of the most important rules for surviving in Kabuki-cho.

Frank nodded at the girls on either side of him, that weird smile still scrunching up his face. His cheeks were turning pink, and I don't think it was only because the room was so warm. It's hard to relax with girls sitting next to you in their underwear, even for guys who go to lingerie pubs all the time. It's not like seeing girls on the beach in bikinis. The swell of breasts in a lacy brassiere, the waistband marks on tummies, the subtle shadow of pubic hair through white panties—unless you're drunk, it seems almost cruel to look and you find yourself averting your eyes. Turning away from the girls and Frank's bashful grin, I fixed my gaze on the computerized tropical fish in a virtual aquarium against the wall. Anyone who didn't know better would have thought the two brilliantly colored angelfish were the real thing. I don't know much about angelfish, but even the way they moved their mouths looked real. There did seem to be something indefinably unnatural about them, though. Like Frank's grin.

"Whiskey-and-water okay?" Reika asked in English. Frank and I nodded, and she poured the unlabeled whiskey into our glasses, then squirted it with water from a siphon.

"Kochira Amerika no kata?" Rie asked, sidling closer to Frank. You weren't allowed to touch the girls in this pub. But sometimes, if you stuck to the rules, the girls themselves would initiate contact. Frank must have caught the word *"Amerika,"* because he turned to Rie and softly said: "Yes."

Afraid that Frank might take the same tiny sips as he had with his beer earlier, I made sure to explain that since the pub worked on a time system he could drink as much whiskey as he liked for the same price. He took tiny sips anyway. You couldn't tell if he was drinking or just wetting his lips, and it was annoying to watch. Reika was sitting on the far side of Frank, and Rie was between him and me. Reika put her hand on Frank's thigh and smiled.

"What's your name?" Frank asked her, and she told him.

"Reika?" he repeated.

"Yes."

"That's a pretty name."

"Really?"

"I think it's very pretty."

"Thank you."

Reika's English was about middle-school level. I'm not a whole lot better, mind you, just more accustomed to using it.

"Do a lot of Americans come here?" Frank asked her.

"Sometimes."

"Your English is good."

"No! I want to speak better, but difficult. I want to get money and go America."

"Oh really? You wanna go to school there?"

"No school! I am stupid! No, I want to go Niketown."

"Niketown?"

"Do you like Nike?"

"Nike? The sporting goods maker?"

"Yes! You like Nike, aren't you?"

"Well, I do have some of their shoes—or wait, maybe mine are Converse. But why do you like Nike so much?"

"No why! I just like. Do you go Niketown?"

"See, I don't know what this Niketown thing is," Frank said. "Do you, Kenji?"

"I've heard of it," I said.

Reika adjusted her bra strap and said: "One big building, many Nike shops! And we can enjoy Nike commercials on giant video screen! My friend said to me. She go to shopping Niketown and buy five, *ano*... ten shoes! Oh! It's my dream, go to shopping Niketown!"

"Your dream?" Frank registered disbelief. "Shopping in Nike stores is your dream?"

"My dream, yes," Reika said and asked him: "Where did you from?"

When he told her New York City, she gave him a funny look.

"Impossible!" she said. "Niketown is in New York."

Naturally, all Reika meant was that she was shocked he could live in New York and not be familiar with her dream store: nothing for Frank to get all bent out of shape about. But his expression underwent the same transformation as when the black tout had ignored him. From where I sat I could clearly see the vinyl-like skin of his cheeks twitching and the capillaries appearing, his face going like a watercolor wash from pink to red. I sensed trouble and turned to Reika, saying: "Only the Japanese make a big deal about Niketown, you'd be surprised how many Americans don't even know about it. I've heard that half the customers are Japanese, and New York is a big place, it's not just Manhattan, you know." I repeated this in English for Frank's benefit. Reika nodded, and Frank's face slowly morphed back to something more or less human. My guess was that Frank was lying about living in New York, but I decided to avoid the subject from then on. Nothing good could come of a guide like me, with no official license, making a customer angry.

"Do you want to karaoke?" Reika asked Frank. One of the other two customers, a middle-aged salaryman, was crooning euphorically into a hand-held mike. He was with a younger colleague, who was drunk and red-faced and humming along, lamely trying to clap in time. In one hand the singer held the mike and in the other the hand of a hostess in pink lingerie. Block out her surroundings, and the hostess might have been holding a sacred flame in a temple in ancient Greece. I figured the two men to be from the sticks. A lot of salarymen from the provinces who visit Tokyo on business trips come to Kabuki-cho at night, probably because it's the one part of town that doesn't put on any airs. It's easy to spot these guys because they always turn bright red when they drink. There's something different about their features, too, not to mention their fashion sense. Untold numbers of them get taken in by hardcore clip joints, and I've often thought guiding tour groups from the farm belt might be profitable. But I'm not about to try to learn all those dialects.

"No karaoke for me," Frank said, "but how about I study some Japanese? I'd like to practice my Japanese with girls in their underwear." He extracted *Tokyo Pink Guide*, the book this time, from his bag.

"The Way of Sexual Liberation!" shouted a blurb on the cover, above the title. Translation: This book will make you horny and show you what to do about it. Below the title it said: "What? Where? And How Much? All the information you need to navigate Tokyo's sexiest spots!" I have a copy of this book for business purposes and am slowly wading through it, partly to brush up my English, but I have to admit it's pretty interesting. For example, Chapter 9 is about the gay scene. It starts with historical background, how the Buddhist prohibitions against women and the machismo of samurai society gave rise to a love of boys, and goes up to the present, taking care to explain that even though the entire sex industry in Japan has developed xenophobia because of AIDS, gays from more enlightened countries are still given a warm welcome in Shinjuku Ni-chome. It even names the best clubs to visit if you happen to be foreign.

Frank opened the bright pink book and looked from Reika to Rie, saying: "All right then, here goes." In the back of the book was a simple Japanese-English sex glossary, and he began reading words in alphabetical order.

"*Aho*," he said in a booming voice, and gave us the English translation (Shithead).

"What did he just say?" Rie asked me, not quite understanding his accent. When I repeated the word, she began laughing and slapping her knee, saying: "*Iya da! Kawaii!*" (I can't stand it! How cute!)

Next Frank read the word *Aijin* (Mistress), then *Ai shiteru* (I love you). He muttered the English translations under his breath, but his voice was loud and resonant when he read the words in Japanese.

"*Aitai* (I want to see you), *Akagai* (Ark shell; Vagina), *Ana* (Hole), *Ana de yaritai* (I want to stick it in), *Anaru sekkusu* (Anal sex), *Asoko* (Down there) . . . *Asoko . . . Asoko . . . Asoko. . . .*"

It's endearing when foreigners try their best to communicate in broken Japanese. When they're giving it all they've got, you find yourself wanting to reward them by comprehending. My English is probably about the level of a decent high-school student's, but I've found that you actually get on better with clients if you struggle to choose the right words rather than try to sound like a native speaker, the way so many idiot Japanese DJs do. As Frank kept repeating *asoko*, Reika and Rie began giggling uncontrollably, and even the other hostesses were turning to see what was so funny. Without the least hint of embarrassment—or lewdness, either—Frank plowed ahead, stumbling over the pronunciations but with an earnest, innocent expression on his face, like an actor on stage, projecting each syllable: *A-SO-KO*.

"*Dai suki* (Love ya!), *Dame* (No!), *Dankon* (Penis), *Danna-san* (Mister), *Dare demo ii desu* (Anyone will do), *Dechatta* (Oops! I came), *Debu* (Fatso), *Dendo kokeshi* (Vibrator), *Desou desu* (I'm going to come), *Doko demo dotei* (A total virgin), *Doko demo dotei dakara desou desu* (I'm a total virgin, so I'm going to come), *Doko demo dotei dakara desou desu, Doko demo dotei dakara desou desu. . . .*"

Frank was noting which phrases got the biggest reaction from Reika and Rie, and these he'd repeat over and over, combining some of them and throwing in other Japanese words he knew. The hostesses sitting unoccupied near the entrance had now stood up to try and hear what Frank was saying, the karaoke singers had put down the mike and were chuckling along with us, and even the two thuggish-looking waiters were enjoying the show. Me, I can't remember the last time I laughed so hard. It literally brought tears to my eyes.

"*Sawaranai* (I won't touch), *Sawaritai* (I want to touch), *Seibyo* (Venereal disease), *Seiko* (Intercourse), *Seiyoku* (Sexual desire), *Senzuri* (Jerking off), *Shakuhachi* (Bamboo flute; Blow job), *Shasei* (Ejaculation), *Shigoku* (To stroke), *Shigoite kudasai* (Please stroke it), *Shigoite kudasai . . . Shigoite kudasai. . . . Sukebe* (Horny bastard), *Sukebe jijii* (Horny old bastard), *Suki desu ka* (Do you like?), *Suki desu* (I like), *Sukebe jijii suki desu ka?* (Do you like horny old bastards?),

Sukebe jijii suki desu (I like horny old bastards) . . . *Sukebe jijii suki desu. . . .*"

The harder we laughed, the more serious Frank looked. He just spoke even louder in order to be heard. Beads of sweat were appearing on Reika and Rie's foreheads and noses and chests, and tears were rolling down their cheeks as they cackled and hiccupped and sputtered. The crooners from the countryside had forgotten all about singing now, and the karaoke track was nearly drowned out by our laughter. Frank, however, continued to observe the ironclad rule of comedians: never laugh at your own stuff. He went on to do almost an hour of this, going back and forth through the entire glossary.

Eventually another pair of customers came in, and the two from the sticks began singing again. The new pair apparently asked for Rie, who moved to their table after shaking Frank's hand and making me tell him she hadn't laughed like that in ages. Reika told Frank: "You are great comedian, I very enjoy!" and slipped away to the restroom to towel off. I was sweating, too, so much that my shirt stuck unpleasantly to my skin. That's what happens when you laugh your ass off in a place where the heat's turned up to accommodate ladies in their underwear. I asked one of the waiters, a guy I knew, for the tab, and he flashed me a smile and said: "That's one fun gaijin!" I won't say you'll only find depressive types working in Kabuki-cho, but everyone there has a past of some kind, not to mention a present that's less than ideal. The employees in this pub probably didn't often get the opportunity to laugh like that, and I was glad they'd enjoyed themselves.

Frank pulled out his wallet and said: "Kenji, what's this Niketown business? Why is it so popular with the Japanese?"

He wasn't sweating at all. I wondered what had made him come out with this question now, so long after the conversation, but I didn't ask. The Japanese like anything that's popular in America, I said.

"I never heard of Niketown," said Frank. "Never knew there was such a place."

"I believe you. It's only here, in this country, that everybody goes crazy over the same things at once."

When the check came, Frank extracted two ¥10,000 notes from his wallet. On one of them was a dark stain, about the size of a large coin, that bothered me a little. It looked like dried blood.

"Frank, I can't remember the last time I laughed so much."

"Really? The girls got a kick out of it too, didn't they?"

"Do you always do things like that?"

"Like what?"

"Make people laugh. I mean, by telling jokes and so on."

"I wasn't trying to be funny. I was just having a Japanese lesson, and then before I knew it it turned into this thing. I still don't really understand what was so hilarious."

We had left the lingerie pub and were walking along the street behind the Koma Theater. It was a little past ten-thirty, and we hadn't yet discussed our next move. I was exhausted from laughing like that, and it had been so hot inside the pub that my only thought was to walk awhile to cool off and settle down. I kept thinking about that ¥10,000 note with what looked like a bloodstain on it. And wondering why it bothered me so much.

"It was a brilliant performance, Frank. Did you study acting or anything?"

"No, but when I was small I had two older sisters who liked that sort of thing. Whenever we had company we used to fool around imitating comedians we'd seen on TV and so forth. But that's about it."

We came to a narrow side street with an atmosphere I've always found kind of eerie. It's like stumbling onto a movie set from the Fifties, a street lined with tiny bars and mahjong parlors, and tea rooms with ivy-grown entrances and classical music playing, all with retro-looking signs out front. One of the bars even had a terra-cotta flowerpot hanging beside the door. The little white flowers shivered in the December wind of Kabuki-cho—a wind ripe with alcohol and sweat and garbage—and reflected the yellow and pink lights of the Koma Theater. Frank seemed to respond to the old-fashioned atmosphere. He stopped at the corner, beneath the simple neon sign of a bar called Auge, and peered into the narrow lane.

"Kenji, there aren't any touts around here."

That, I explained, was because anyone walking this way would already have decided exactly where he was going. On this street you didn't get the drunken sorts roving arm in arm with their buddies, checking out all the clubs and looking for the cheapest and easiest place to get their rocks off.

"This is the way Kabuki-cho used to look," I said.

"Is that so? I guess it's the same in every town." Frank started walking again. "Times Square in New York was like this, way back when—used to be lots of nice bars before the sex shops moved in."

He said this in such a nostalgic way that I decided he really was a New Yorker after all. It was silly to expect everyone from New York to know about Niketown.

"Speaking of which, Kenji, I saw a building in front of Shinjuku Station with a big sign saying 'Times Square,' but—what is that, some kind of joke?"

"No," I said. "It's the name of a department store."

"But Times Square is Times Square because the old Times Tower was there. The *New York Times* doesn't have a building in Shinjuku, does it?"

"Japanese think using names like that is cool."

"Well, it's not cool, it's embarrassing. Japan may have lost the war, but that was a long time ago now. Why keep imitating America?"

I didn't have an answer for that, so I just asked Frank where he wanted to go next. He said he wanted to try a peep show, to see girls who were completely nude.

We had to retrace our steps a bit. There are no peep shows around Kuyakusho Avenue, just Chinese clubs and girlie bars and pub-restaurants and love hotels. We turned the corner at a love hotel to head back toward Seibu Shinjuku Station and found ourselves walking past a rent-a-car lot. What it was doing in a place like that I couldn't tell you. Who in the world would come here to rent a car? There isn't even room on the streets to park. The

Toyota Rent-a-Car banner and the strings of vinyl pennants flapped in the wind, and the prefab office was all but hidden among the dozen or so dust-covered station wagons and sedans squeezed fender to fender inside the tiny lot. I'd rather walk any day than drive something like that, I thought. Frank was shuffling along with his collar turned up and his hands stuffed in his pockets. The tip of his nose was red. He had no coat or muffler and the warmth from the lingerie pub had faded quickly enough, but he didn't look cold so much as dejected. I looked over at him as we walked past the Toyota lot, and a chill trickled down my spine. It was something about his posture in silhouette. He gave off this overpowering, almost tangible loneliness.

All Americans have something lonely about them. I don't know what the reason for that might be, except maybe that they're all descended from immigrants. But Frank had taken it to a whole new level. His cheap clothing and slovenly appearance had something to do with it: shorter even than my 172 centimeters, he was fat, his hair was combed forward and thinning, and right now he looked very old for his age. But it wasn't just that. There was a falseness about him, as if his whole existence was somehow made up. That's what I was thinking, anyway, when I noticed something that made my scalp crawl. Just ahead was a trash collection site cordoned off with yellow tape, and a cop was standing guard. This was where the schoolgirl's corpse had been found.

Things that had been tugging at my brain merged with the trickling chill. Something in that newspaper article about all the cash having been removed from the murdered girl's wallet. The bloodstained ¥10,000 note Frank had whipped out at the lingerie pub. And the fact that Frank had said he imported Toyota parts and yet hadn't shown the least interest in the rows of Toyotas we'd just passed.

I told myself these were just random, unconnected blips, but I couldn't shake my suspicion, and before I knew it I was getting all worked up. I had to keep telling myself to calm down and be reasonable. It's crazy to suspect a guy of murder just because he lied about his job and has a bill stained with something that looks like blood. And maybe he wasn't lying about his job but only cares about the parts he imports, not the whole car. That's what I kept telling myself, but I wished I could hear it from someone else. If someone would tell me, even over the phone, that I was letting my imagination run away with me, maybe that would be enough to pull me out of it. The only person I could think of was Jun.

"Um, it's almost eleven o'clock," I told Frank, showing him my watch. "We agreed on three hours, right? Till midnight?"

"Oh, that's right. But we're having so much fun, and I'm just getting warmed up. What do you say, Kenji? Would you mind going a couple of hours extra?"

"Well, actually," I said, "I kind of promised my girlfriend..."

Frank furrowed his brow, and I could see the light going out of his eyes. Shit, I thought, here comes the Face.

"But, then again," I said, "work comes first! I'll just give her a call."

I marched toward a phone booth across from the Koma Theater. I didn't want to use my mobile. I was pretty sure Frank didn't understand any Japanese to speak of, but I still didn't like the idea of him standing beside me listening. It was a relief to get the glass walls of the booth between us. Jun was generally in my room around this time of night. Not that she was waiting for me to get back—she likes to spend time there by herself, reading or listening to music, because she doesn't have any private space at home. Jun's parents divorced when she was small, and she lives with her mother and little brother. She tells her mother she's been studying at a friend's house, and as long as she gets home by midnight no questions are asked.

"Hello? Oh, hi, Kenji." I felt another wave of relief just hearing her voice, which is pretty low and husky for a sixteen-year-old girl.

"Hi. What're you doing?"

"Just listening to the radio."

Jun's mother works in the sales department of an insurance company, and I know Jun loves her a lot and appreciates everything she's done for her. The apartment the three of them share in Takaido has only two rooms and a kitchen, but with her mother working late every night just to make ends meet, Jun can hardly suggest they move to a bigger place. I met Jun in Kabuki-cho. She wasn't selling it, but she was doing some compensated dating in those days. Going with middle-aged guys to dinner or karaoke, for which she'd get from five to twenty thousand yen. We don't talk about that very much.

"I'm still working."

"Poor thing, it's cold out there! I made some risotto. It's in the pot."

"Thanks, Jun. You know, this client of mine is kind of weird."

"Weird how?"

"I don't know, he... He's a liar."

"You mean he won't pay what he promised?"

"No, it's not that. He just seems suspicious."

I gave her the basic facts about the bloodstained bill and the Toyota thing.

"So you think he's a killer?" she said. "Just because of that?"

"I'm crazy, right?"

"Well, I haven't seen him, but..."

"What?"

"I think I know what you mean."

"About what?"

"Well, the way that girl was murdered—it was pretty over the top, right? I was thinking it didn't seem like the way a Japanese would kill somebody. What's he doing right now?"

My eyes had been on Frank the whole time. He'd watched me for a while, then got bored and wandered over to the game center across the street and stood loitering in front of it.

"He's checking out a Print Club booth."

"A what?"

"You know, that machine that takes photos of you and then prints them out on cute little stickers. I don't think he knows how it works. He's watching a group of girls posing for a picture."

"I think you're probably all right, then, Kenji. I can't imagine a murderer making Print Club photos of himself."

I'm not sure why, but that seemed to make sense.

"Kenji," she said, "take some photos with the guy. I want to see what he looks like."

I said I would and hung up.

"What is this thing, Kenji? Those girls sure seemed to be enjoying themselves. I think it took their picture. Is it one of those passport photo machines?"

I started to explain, but a drunken office worker was standing behind us with his girlfriend, whose face could have stopped a train, urging us to hurry up. Normally I would have made some snappy reply, but I was preoccupied with Frank and it was cold and all I said was: "All right, just give us a minute here." I decided to skip the explanation and just take a picture. Frank said he didn't have any change, so I paid. I stood him in front of the machine and was selecting the background he'd chosen—the Japanesy one, a *yakitori* stand —when he insisted we pose for it together.

"Those girls all took pictures together, I want one with you and me."

To take a Print Club two-shot, you need to put your faces right next to each other. I'm not saying Frank revolted me, but I wasn't about to press my cheek against his. Just the fact that he was a man made it bad enough, but Frank also had that weird skin. No wrinkles, though he was supposedly in his mid-thirties, but his face wasn't what you'd call smooth, either—it was shiny and flabby and artificial-looking. At any rate, it wasn't a face I wanted touching mine, but Frank put his arm around my shoulder, pulled me close, spun toward the screen and said: "Okay, Kenji, shoot!"

Frank's cheek was cold and felt like the silicone they use in diving masks.

"Hey, man, I heard this gaijin of yours is a real scream."

Passing the lingerie pub, I ran into Satoshi again. "At this time of night it's only ¥7000 apiece, absolutely no extra charges!" he was bellowing to the drunks stumbling by. Watching him, I felt I understood what he meant about

Kabuki-cho being "easy." There's an anything-goes feeling to the place, no "normal" standard of behavior to live up to and no illusions of glory or shame. You either get your money or you get fired and move on. Frank had stopped walking a few paces back and was studying the photo strips.

"Did the waiter say anything about him?" I asked Satoshi. "Like, about the money he paid with?"

"No, why?"

Apparently I was the only one getting stressed over the stain on that bill. I decided to forget about it. I didn't need Jun to tell me I was being paranoid. The coincidence of seeing the very spot where the schoolgirl's corpse had been dumped, immediately after passing that ghostly rent-a-car place, must have made my nerves short out in some way. At least that's how I decided to look at it.

"He wants to go to a peep show," I told Satoshi. "Heard about any good ones lately?"

"Hey, man, they're all the same," Satoshi laughed, then added, after glancing back at Frank: "Times are tough all around." Translation: That's one sorry-looking excuse for a customer you're dragging around, man.

The nearest peep show was on the sixth floor of the building right in front of us.

"No, Kenji." Frank shook his head. "I need you to come in with me."

I'd led him up to the entrance to the club and told him I'd wait outside to save him money, but Frank insisted on buying admission for two: ¥5000. The show had just begun, so we had to sit on a small sofa next to the reception counter and wait. They don't let you walk in during a show, but the shows only last about ten minutes. On the wall was a collection of photos from when the club had been featured on a late-night TV program. The pictures were pretty old: the colors were faded, and the celebrity reporter's autograph was disappearing.

"Did your girlfriend understand about you working late?" Frank asked me.

He was looking at a sign on the wall that said, in both Japanese and English: THIS IS A TOP QUALITY PEEP SHOW THAT WAS SHOWN ON TELEVISION.

"Sure. No problem."

"That's good. So what's the system in this place?"

Music from the show filtered out to where we sat. I didn't know the title, but it was a Diana Ross song. I explained. Most shows last three or four songs. A girl comes out and takes off her clothes, and meanwhile, as the show is starting, a different woman comes to your booth and asks if you want the "special service."

Frank said: "Special service?"

"Hand job. Which will cost an extra ¥3000."

This got a definite rise out of Frank.

"Hand job," he murmured and peered off into the distance, or the distant past. I'd never heard anyone say the words with such feeling before. You don't have to get one if you don't want one, I told him.

"Since you're aiming to get laid tonight, you may not want a hand job first."

"Oh, that's all right," Frank said and looked at me. "My sex drive is pretty strong. In fact, I'm a sexual superman."

Sexual superman. Those were his exact words.

"In that case, when the woman comes to the booth and asks you something, all you need to do is say 'Yes.' "

"All right, then," Frank said, "I will. I can't wait."

For someone who couldn't wait he looked awfully bored. He sighed and picked up a weekly magazine next to the sofa. On the first page of color photos was a picture of Hideo Nomo in his Los Angeles Dodgers uniform. The short text was about the contract for Nomo's second season not having been signed yet. Frank tapped the picture with his forefinger and said:

"So baseball's pretty big in Japan too, I guess?"

At first I thought he was making a joke. There's no such thing as an American who comes to Japan on business and doesn't know who Nomo is. Not even one in a thousand. Among Americans he's surely the most famous Japanese alive, and right now small talk about Nomo is probably the best way to break the ice and get negotiations off to a smooth start. And yet Frank was looking at a picture of Nomo and assuming he played in Japan. Was it even possible that a man who imported Toyota auto parts wouldn't know who Nomo was?

"This man pitches for the Los Angeles Dodgers," I said.

Frank peered at the photo dubiously.

"You're right, he's wearing a Dodgers uniform."

"It's Nomo. He's famous. Last year he pitched a no-hit, no-run game."

Maybe Frank didn't know anything at all about baseball. That was the only way this could make any sense to me—if he knew nothing about the game itself. But then he pulled the rug out again.

"No-hit, no-run, eh? That takes me back. We were all boys in my family, a gang of brothers. I was the youngest, but all of us played baseball. We lived way out in the country, you understand, cornfields as far as the eye could see, and in summer we used to do nothing but play catch. There wasn't much else to do, for one thing, and my father was a baseball fan too. I still remember the summer I was eight years old, when my second oldest brother pitched a no-hit, no-run game."

Just an hour earlier, Frank had told me he had two older sisters. These two sisters, I distinctly remembered him saying, used to imitate TV comedians. But now he came from a family of only boys who all played baseball. The weird thing was that there was no conceivable need for him to lie right now. It was odd that he didn't know who Nomo was, but no reason to initiate a coverup. This wasn't a conference room where vital business talks were taking place, it was the waiting room outside a peep show, and I wasn't some important client or supplier but just a nightlife guide. If he had simply said, "Nomo, eh? Never heard of him," I probably wouldn't have thought twice about it.

"It was the middle of nowhere, but they made good beer there, and we used to all play baseball and then drink beer. I was just a kid but of course they made me drink too because you couldn't call yourself a man if you couldn't knock back a beer. That's what it's like in the countryside in America, cornfields stretching forever in every direction, the sky so blue it's shocking, and unbelievably hot in summer. The sun is like a hammer pounding you down, and a weak man could pass out from just standing there. But the amazing thing was, when we were playing baseball the heat didn't bother us at all, it didn't even seem that hot. Even if the pitcher was getting bombed and we were stuck out in the field for a long time, even then we didn't notice the heat."

Frank seemed excited by these memories, if that's what they were, and was speaking much faster than normal. I tried to concentrate, to make sure I didn't miss anything, but at some point I started remembering my own younger days. I played baseball in middle school. Our team wasn't very good, but I've never forgotten those summer practice sessions or the games we played. What Frank had just said was true: even on days when it was so hot you could hardly bear to be outside, you forgot all about it once you started playing. For anybody who's had the experience, those two words "summer" and "baseball" are bound to summon up the smells of grass and dirt and oiled leather. It made me so nostalgic I completely forgot that Frank was almost certainly lying.

"I know," I said. "When your team's fielding, and you're leading by a couple of runs, and it's two outs bases loaded, you don't notice how hot it is. But if you close your eyes for a second, suddenly you realize it's like being inside an oven. In fact, that's the hottest I've ever been. There's no heat like the heat you experience playing baseball in summer. And there's no memory more beautiful."

I had launched into this little soliloquy without even thinking. I was enjoying my own reminiscences, and it all came bubbling out fairly smoothly. I didn't have to stop and think about present perfect or comparative degree or whatever.

"So you played baseball too, Kenji?" Frank asked without much enthusiasm.

"Yeah. Yes I did."

I was glad to be able to say that. And now that I thought about it, Frank had probably grown up in a complicated family situation, one that a Japanese like me would find difficult to comprehend. We often see magazine articles about the divorce rate in America being over fifty percent or something, but that doesn't give us a real sense of what it's like. We just think, Hmm, how about that, and turn the page. But I'd worked as a nightlife guide for nearly two hundred Americans so far, and when it came time to say goodbye after hanging out with them for a couple of nights, more than a few would start drunkenly telling me about their childhoods. This is especially true of guys who hadn't managed to find the kind of sex they wanted with the kind of woman they liked—which is almost everyone, since there's not much chance of going to a foreign country for two or three days and finding a woman you like and having sex with her. I think that's part of the reason so many of my clients, after wandering through the long Tokyo night, end up drunk and tired and determined to confess their loneliness to me. Because of my father dying when I was a kid, I do feel like I understand to some extent when they talk about their sense of loss or whatever, but still. This is the sort of story I'd hear, for example: *Pop stopped coming home, and then the next year at Christmas there was a man I didn't know, and my mother said from now on this is your father. I was only six so I didn't have much choice in the matter, but it took me a long time to accept it, two or three years about, and then at some point the man started hitting me. This was back in North Carolina, and we had a custom where we didn't mow or walk on the grass until May, to let it grow, and the man was a salesman from the West Coast and didn't know about that, so he used to walk all over the lawn in front of the house in early spring, and Pop had planted that lawn, so it really upset me, and I warned the man, I told him again and again, but he kept walking on the grass, and finally I called him this really bad name, which I must have just learned because I didn't even know what it meant. That was the first time he hit me, and then I had to start all over again, trying to get to a point where I could, you know . . . accept it.*

I remember the American making this particular confession, and the way his voice caught when he said "accept it." Americans don't talk about just grinning and bearing it, which is the Japanese approach to so many things. After listening to a lot of these stories, I began to think that American loneliness is a completely different creature from anything we experience in this country, and it made me glad I was born Japanese. The type of loneliness where you need to keep struggling to accept a situation is fundamentally different from the sort you know you'll get through if you just hang in there. I don't think I could stand the sort of loneliness Americans feel.

I was sure Frank had a similar sad story. Who knows—maybe he was a foster child who got bounced around from home to home. At one time he might have been in a household with only older sisters, and later in one with only older brothers.

"I played in middle school, second base," I said. "The shortstop and I were best friends. I had a pretty good arm for a second baseman, and he had a good arm too, and we used to practice double plays a lot. In fact, double plays were everything to us. Like, even if we lost a game, if we managed to turn a double play we'd give each other the thumbs up when no one was looking."

After spilling out this little reverie, I asked Frank what position he had played, but just then the previous show finished and an announcement came over the speakers: We're sorry to have kept you waiting, please enter the booths, please enter the booths. "It must be our turn, Kenji, let's go," Frank said abruptly and stood up. I stood up too and moved toward the door to the booths, but I was fuming. The bastard gets all pumped up talking about baseball, and then when I try to join in he suddenly loses interest and seems anxious to drop the subject altogether.

We were led to separate booths some distance apart. For a guy who claimed to have such a strong sex drive, Frank didn't look all that eager to get into his booth. Not that he seemed nervous, just uncomfortable and bored. What a weird guy, I muttered under my breath as I entered my own little cubicle.

It was furnished with a round stool and a box of tissues and was so narrow I was glad I wasn't claustrophobic.

The show started right away. As in most of these places, the stage was a half circle no more than two meters across, separated from the booths by one-way mirrors. The dancer can't see inside the booths, but she can tell which ones are occupied, thanks to a little light in the wall above each mirror. The music started, and the cheesiest illumination imaginable began to glitter as a door opened in the right rear of the stage and a small, skinny girl walked out. The music was something by Michael Jackson. The girl was wearing a negligee.

There was a knock, and someone opened the door to my booth and poked her head inside.

"Excuse me. Would you like the special service?" She peered at my face, then said: "What the hell, if it isn't Kenji."

About six months ago she'd been working at a show pub in Roppongi, and her name, if I remembered right, was Asami.

"Asami?" I said, and she laughed and told me they called her Madoka here.

"Listen," I said, "I've got a favor to ask you. Three booths down from here is a gaijin who's going to want the special service."

As soon as Asami/Madoka heard the word "gaijin," she creased her brow in a frown. Like I said, the popularity of foreigners in the sex industry has completely bottomed out.

"Don't get me wrong. I'm not going to ask you to give him something extra or anything. I just want to know if he, um, ejaculates a lot. Quantity-wise, I mean."

"What? What is it, a contest or something?"

"No, I just want to know. Humor me. I'll treat you to dinner sometime."

"All right," Madoka said and shut the door. I had requested her as a hostess at the Roppongi show pub a few times, and girls in the sex trade remember that sort of thing. What I was asking of her now sounded crazy, I know. But the newspaper had said that the dismembered high-school girl showed signs of having been sexually assaulted. She'd been killed less than two days before, and I figured if Frank was the one who raped her, he probably wouldn't have much semen stored up yet. Of course, it was crazy for me to suspect Frank of having anything to do with the murdered girl in the first place. I was thinking too much, is what Jun, for example, would probably tell me. But after two years of working Tokyo's sex scene I'd developed a sort of sixth sense for danger, and even if Frank wasn't a murderer my intuition was definitely telling me not to trust him. Everybody lies at one time or another. But once someone makes a habit of lying, once it becomes a part of their everyday life, denial kicks in. Even the fact that they're lying begins to fade into the background, and in extreme cases they actually forget. I know more than a few people like that, and I make sure to steer clear of them, because they're the world's biggest pains in the ass. Not to mention dangerous.

On stage, the small, thin woman was opening the front of her negligee and gyrating her hips. She wasn't a professional dancer, just another girl in the sex industry, so there was nothing very seductive about her moves. Comical and sad, is more like it, but nobody had come to this place expecting to see an artistic striptease. The woman pressed against the one-way mirror before each booth for about thirty seconds, giving the customers what they'd come for by pulling down her bra and squeezing her breasts, sticking her finger down her panties, and so on. She wasn't wearing much makeup, and her skin was so pale you could see the veins in her face and arms and legs. There was something cruel about the way the cheap illumination highlighted those blue veins, I was thinking, when Madoka opened the door to my booth again and stuck her head inside.

"Well?" I said quietly. A wave of strong perfume washed over me. Madoka was wearing a sort of negligee with frills, looking for all the world as if she were off in search of the bluebird of happiness. She was also holding a vinyl bag full of condoms and moist towelettes.

"The ... the gaijin in Booth 5, right?" she said.

"I don't remember the booth number, but surely there's only one gaijin here?" The booths are dark, and with the light behind her it was hard to see

Madoka's face, but she sounded troubled, as if she didn't know what to say. "Didn't he ask for the special service?"

Madoka shook her head and said: "No, he *did*, but..."

"Did something weird happen?"

"He stopped me after a while and said 'No more.'"

"So he didn't come?"

"That's not what I mean...."

"How big was he?"

"Size-wise, about average I think, but... Something wasn't right. First of all, I've never seen anybody make a face like that when they're getting jerked off. And his dingaling was, like... creepy."

"Creepy."

"Yeah. It was hard in some places and soft in others."

"Silicone injections?"

"No. I could tell if it was silicone or pearls or whatever, but this was different. And that face! At first it was dark and I couldn't see very well, but then a light shone on his face, and it was like, I mean, he was looking at me, but... Can I go now? I get yelled at for talking to customers."

"Of course, sorry to ask such a weird favor," I said, and Madoka said no problem and shut the door again. She didn't seem to want to talk about Frank. The girl on stage, braless now, had her panties down around one ankle and was masturbating. She lay on her back with her legs spread and her eyes closed, moaning softly. No one but she herself could have said if it was just an act, or if she was actually a bit turned on, or if in fact she was the type who really gets off on having people watch. I certainly didn't know which it was, but her voice and facial expressions were a pretty good facsimile of what happens when a woman is genuinely aroused. There's not that much variation, which I'm sure is true for men too. Someone like Madoka has seen the faces of hundreds, if not thousands, of men in that state. What sort of face could Frank have made that she'd find so disturbing?

After we left the peep show Frank hardly spoke at all, and I didn't much feel like talking either. We just walked along, drifting away from the neon lights and the cries of the touts, and the next thing I knew we were in front of a batting center on the outskirts of the love hotel district. It was past 1:00 A.M., but we could hear a syncopated clank of metal bats beyond the tall green net and rusty chain-link fence. Frank stopped to listen to the sound, and gazed curiously up at the fence. I'm told that in America they don't fence in batting centers or driving ranges. I'd always assumed that enclosed driving ranges, at least, were something you could find anywhere in the world. I thought that vending machines for booze and cigarettes and magazines and whatnot were everywhere, too. Well, maybe not everywhere, but it never occurred to me that having vending machines for beer or whatever on every other corner was unusual. Clients with any curiosity always ask me about this, though. Kenji, why are there so many vending machines? Who needs them, with convenience stores everywhere you turn? And why do you need so many different types of canned coffee and juice and sports drinks? With so many brands, how can anyone possibly make a profit? I've never been able to come up with answers to questions like these, and at first I didn't even understand what the big deal was. But from the point of view of foreigners, any number of things about this country seem abnormal, and I'm not able to explain most of them. I get questions like: If Japan is one of the richest countries in the world, why do you have this *karoshi* problem, people literally working themselves to death? Or: Girls from poor Asian countries I can understand, but why do high-school girls in a country as wealthy as Japan prostitute themselves? Or: Wherever you go in the world, people work in order to make their families happy, so why doesn't anybody in Japan complain about the *tanshin-funin* system that sends businessmen off to live on their own in distant cities or countries? If I can't answer these questions, it's not because I'm particularly stupid. Nobody writes about these things in the newspapers or weeklies, or talks about them on TV. No one teaches us why *karoshi* has to exist in this country, or the *tanshin-funin* system that the rest of the world seems to think is so perverse.

Frank stood riveted to one spot, gazing up at the batting center. I thought maybe he'd enjoy hitting a few. "Wanna try it?" I said, and he looked at me as if startled and bobbled his head ambiguously.

On the ground floor was a game center. We climbed a metal staircase to the second level, a surreal open space illuminated by fluorescent lights. A sign hanging about midway up the chain-link fence said: FOR YOUR SAFETY, ONLY THOSE TAKING BATTING PRACTICE ARE ALLOWED IN THE CAGES. There were seven batting cages, all set at different pitching speeds. The one farthest to the right was the fastest, 135 kph, and the one on the far left was the slowest at 80. Two of the cages were occupied—one by a young man in training wear and the other by the male half of a drunken couple. His woman was egging him on. "Go for a home run!" she shouted before every pitch. The man was staggering drunk and missed most of the balls completely, but the woman kept at him as if their lives depended on it: "Don't let 'em beat you! Don't let 'em beat you!" Don't ask me who or what was trying to beat him. She stood behind the fence on a long concrete walkway like the platforms you see at little train stations in the country, with a roof but no walls to block the wind. In a shed about the size of a highway tollbooth the batting center attendant slumped in his chair, asleep, and next to him a kettle sat on a small kerosene stove that flickered with orange flames. The little shed must have been warm, because the dozing attendant inside had nothing on over his T-shirt, and a homeless man lay with his back against the outer wall. He was sprawled out on a couple of flattened cardboard boxes, drinking some colorless liquor from a Cup Noodle container and leafing through a magazine.

"There's no place like this in America," Frank said.

I didn't think there were many places like it in Japan, either. The pitching machines were lined up in the shadows of a sort of bunker, and small green lights blinked at the tips of the two catapult arms that were currently operating. Hit or miss, the balls rolled down to a conveyor belt that carried them back to the machines. Intermittently, between the beats of a Yuki Uchida song crackling over the primitive loudspeakers, you could hear the rumbling of the conveyor belt and the creaking of the machines as they wound the arm-springs tighter and tighter. The guy in training wear was dripping with sweat and hitting the ball pretty good. Of course, no matter how well he connected, the ball couldn't go any farther than the netting, about twenty meters away. High up on the net was an oval cloth banner that said HOME RUN, except that the cloth was ripped and the "M" was missing.

"You wanna hit some?" I asked Frank again.

"I'm kind of tired," he said. "I think I'll just rest awhile. Why don't you hit some, Kenji, and I'll watch. Go ahead, take a few swings."

Frank dragged a metal lawn chair over from in front of the attendant's shed to sit on. As he did so, the homeless guy looked at him, and Frank asked him in English: "Is anyone using this chair?" The homeless guy didn't answer but took another sip of his vodka or *shochu* or whatever it was. I could smell the booze from where I stood, not to mention the stink of the man himself.

"Is this where he lives?" Frank asked, looking over at the guy as he sat down.

"I'm sure he doesn't live here, no."

I was freezing and wanted to hit some balls to warm up but felt awkward about asking Frank to pay for it. I enjoy swinging a bat, and it was only ¥300 a turn, so I could have paid for myself easily enough, but it wasn't for my sake that I'd led Frank up those metal stairs. I'll admit I was tired of walking, but really we were only here because Frank had said all that stuff about playing baseball as a kid. This was part of my job—trying to see that he enjoyed himself. Besides, I still hadn't recouped my ¥300 for the Print Club photos. Not a lot, I know, but it was the principle of the thing. I'd told him at the outset that the client has to bear all expenses, and it wasn't in my interest to have him start thinking of me as a buddy—that wouldn't do at all. Maybe it was the strange exhaustion I felt that made me incapable of asking him to get change. I was strangely exhausted.

"He's homeless, right?" Frank said.

"That's right, yeah."

I felt like I was coming down with a cold, and I didn't want to stand there in the wind chatting. Behind us was a parking lot, and through the links in the fence you could see the neon signs of all the love hotels. Frank, his nose red from the cold he didn't seem to feel, sank deeply into the lawn chair and just sat there watching the bum sip his liquor.

"Why doesn't somebody chase him out of here?"

"Too much trouble."

"I saw a lot of homeless in the park too, and in the station. I didn't realize there were so many in Japan. Are there kids here who rough them up?"

"Yeah, there are," I said, thinking: Doesn't this clown realize how cold it is?

"I bet there are. So what do you think of kids who'd do such a thing, Kenji?"

"Stuff like that is going to happen, I guess. They smell bad, for one thing. It's hard to imagine wanting to get close and be nice to them."

"The smell, huh? That's true, smell is definitely a factor in deciding who we like and don't like. New York has street gangs that specialize in molesting vagrants. No money in it of course, they just take pleasure in the violence, pulling a homeless fellow's teeth out one by one with pliers, for example, or even assaulting them sexually."

Why was Frank carrying on about things like this, in a place like this, at a time like this? The don't-let-'em-beat-you woman was now helping her defeated warrior stumble off toward the stairs. The guy in the training wear was still batting. It was so cold on that windblown platform I felt as if I were naked below the waist and standing on a block of ice. Most of the windows in the love hotels had lights on. Looking up at those dim, sleazy lights I remembered what Madoka had told me in the peep show booth. *I've never seen anybody make a face like that when they're getting jerked off.* Come to think of it, she never actually told me whether Frank had come or not, let alone the quantity. Not that it seemed to matter at this point. What sort of face could he have made, though?

"You don't like this kind of talk, do you," Frank said, his eyes still on the homeless guy.

I shook my head, thinking: If you can tell that, how about putting a lid on it?

"I wonder why. I guess because to talk about it makes you picture it, and nobody wants a picture in their mind of kids beating the crap out of a bum who stinks to high heaven. But why is it that if you imagine a baby who smells of milk, for example, you can't help smiling? Why is there such agreement around the world about what is or isn't a foul smell? Who decided what smells bad? Is it impossible that somewhere in this world there are people who, if they sat next to a homeless fellow they'd get an urge to snuggle up to him, but if they sat next to a baby they'd get an urge to kill it? Something tells me there must be people like that somewhere, Kenji."

Listening to Frank talk like this made me feel queasy. "I'm gonna hit a few," I said, and put the fence between us.

I stepped into the batting cage marked "100 kph." The floor was concrete and slightly sloping so the balls would collect at the bottom, near the machines, and the concrete was painted white but took on a bluish tinge in the fluorescent lights. Beyond the net all you could see were the neon signs of the love hotels and their sad, dimly lit windows. I stretched briefly, thinking: Could the view possibly be any bleaker? I selected the lightest of the three available bats and put three coins in the slot. The pitching machine's green light came on, I heard the low rumble of the motor, and before I knew it a white ball came zipping out of the long, narrow darkness. Even a hundred kilometers an hour is pretty fast, and I wasn't really ready, so I missed the first ball completely.

My next few swings weren't much better. I couldn't get a solid hit, kept fouling the ball off, and Frank sat back there staring at me. Finally he got up from the chair and walked this way. He clung to the fence and said: "Kenji, what's the matter, you haven't hit one past home plate!"

For some reason this really pissed me off. I didn't want to hear shit like that from someone like him.

"Watch *that* fellow." Frank rolled his eyes toward the guy in training wear, two cages up. "He's banging the heck out of 'em."

This was true. The guy was nailing almost every pitch—at 120 kph—and lining them all toward center. His bat speed wasn't something you see every day. I figured him for a pro of sorts, maybe employed as a ringer for a team in the early morning leagues. I'd heard you could find such specimens in Kabuki-cho: guys who, after starring on high-school or corporate teams, get into trouble with women or gambling or drugs and, not having any other way to make money, become paid secret weapons in the amateur leagues. They're on a piecework basis—¥2000 for a home run, ¥500 for a hit, or whatever—so they need to stay in practice.

"I've been watching you this whole time, Kenji. You haven't hit the ball cleanly even once yet, and these pitches are a lot slower than his are."

"I know that," I said, a little more loudly than necessary. I took a huge swing at the next ball and missed. Frank groaned and shook his head.

"Oh my God, what was that? And such an easy pitch!"

That did it. I stepped away and took a few practice swings, trying to focus. Frank was back there muttering that it must be a curse, that even God had abandoned me, or something along those lines.

"Will you be quiet, please!" I shouted. "How am I supposed to concentrate with you talking like that?"

Frank sighed and shook his head again.

"Kenji, do you know the story about Jack Nicklaus? Very famous story. Jack had a long putt to decide some major tournament, you see, and he was standing over the ball concentrating so hard that he didn't even notice it when the wind blew his hat off. Now *that's* concentration."

"Jack who?" I said. "Never heard of him. Just be quiet, all right? If you'll just be quiet, I'll hit that home run sign for you."

"Hmph," Frank snorted. Then, nodding slowly, his face a blank mask, he said: "Wanna bet?"

The way he said it really got to me. Maybe Frank pulled this kind of stunt all the time, I thought. Maybe all the needling had been calculated to lead up to that final line: *Hmph. Wanna bet?* Looking at that poker face of his I found myself thinking he just might be the sort of scumbag who would stoop to something like that. But it was already too late.

"Fine with me."

I was saying these words before I even realized it. That cool, clear judgment I pride myself on, so rare in a guy my age, got clouded by the rage Frank's droopy, no-expression face triggered in me.

"Here's what we'll do, Kenji," he said. "You get twenty balls, and if you hit even one home run out of the twenty, you win and I'll pay you double your fee for tonight. But if you don't hit a home run, I win and I don't owe you anything."

You're on, I almost said, but stopped myself.

"Frank, that's not fair."

"Why not?"

"If you win, all my work this evening adds up to nothing. Zero. You don't have a zero option, which means I'm risking more than you."

"So how do you want it?"

"If you win you only have to pay half the fee, and if I win you pay double the fee. That's logical, right?"

"Then if you win I pay you the ¥20,000 basic rate plus the ¥20,000 for two hours extra, that's ¥40,000 times two, total of ¥80,000?"

That's right, I said, a little taken aback that he'd remembered the payment system so accurately. He's an American all right, I thought. Americans never forget the original agreement. No matter how drunk they get or how many naked ladies they get excited about, they always remember.

"Talk about not fair—that means if you win you're ahead ¥40,000 but if I win I'm only ahead ¥20,000." He stared into my eyes for a beat, then said: "You're a cheapskate."

I don't know if this was meant as a challenge to sucker me in or what, but it worked.

"All right, the original conditions you stated," I said, and Frank twisted his lips into a smile.

"I'll pay for this one, Kenji," he said. He took a coin purse from the inner breast pocket of his jacket and picked out three ¥100 coins. His fingernails were longish and jagged and not overly clean. I took the coins, thinking: If he had change, why didn't he pull it out at the photo booth?

"How many balls do you get for ¥300?"

"Thirty," I said.

"All right, then, the first ten will be just for practice, and the bet starts with ball number eleven."

I was convinced that Frank had planned all this. It was becoming obvious what a crafty bastard he was. Maybe he'd been watching the probably semipro guy two cages down smashing them consistenty toward center and still never hitting the home run banner. When I first came up to Tokyo from Shizuoka I went to a prep school for about four months and had a part-time job delivering packages. Often, though, when the weather was nice and I had some time off, I'd go to a batting center alongside the Tama River, just a couple of train stops from my apartment. They had a home run sign, too, and if you hit it you'd win a prize—your choice of a teddy bear or vouchers for beer, as I recall. One day I hit more than a hundred balls, but I never did hit that sign, and only once did I ever see anyone else hit it. The sign, about the size of a small surfboard, was hung maybe fifteen meters up the netting and twenty meters from the batting box, and there was no way you could hit it with a line drive. The one ball I saw graze the sign at Tama River for a teddy bear was a blooping pop fly hit by some housewife.

The pitching machine growled to life. I went through the first ten practice balls in what seemed like no time. I was trying to keep my shoulders and arms relaxed and to concentrate on hitting the ball cleanly. That's what Dad used to tell me when he first taught me how to play baseball, when I was seven or eight. My father helped design machinery for public works projects and was sent overseas a lot, mostly to Southeast Asia. His health wasn't that great, but he enjoyed both watching and playing sports. Keep your eye on the ball—that's what he kept telling me when he'd bought me my first mitt and took me outside to play catch.

I managed to really tag it on my first official swing, smashing a line drive up the middle, and heard Frank behind me go: "Whoa." But the ball hit the netting about two meters below the home run sign. I connected well with the next one too, but it was even lower and banged against the steel mesh protecting the pitching machines. Every time I told myself to keep my eye on the ball, it conjured up a picture of Dad. I don't remember him playing with me that much—he was out of town more often than not, and ended up spending most of his time in Malaysia, where he was helping build a big bridge. But even now I often dream that I'm playing catch with him.

On the third pitch I lined one that would have been good for extra bases, right down the third-base line and nowhere near the home run banner. On the fourth and fifth I hit grounders. After about ten of my twenty pitches, I was so focused on the ball that I'd forgotten all about Frank, but my head was full of my father. My mother seems to have considered him something of a playboy, but that sort of thing doesn't matter to you when you're a kid. "I have two regrets," Dad said when he was dying of lung disease: "Not seeing that bridge completed, and not teaching Kenji how to swim." Apparently when I was born he told himself that though he'd probably be too busy to play with his son much, at the very least he'd teach me the fundamentals of baseball and swimming. I sometimes think my desire to go to America may have a lot to do with him. He always looked so happy, after having come home for a brief stay, to be heading back to Malaysia. My mother says it was because he had a "local floozy" there, but I don't think that could have been the only reason. Maybe he did have a woman, and I know he loved his work, but I also think there was something about Malaysia itself that excited him. It was sad when he left, of course, but my father was never more appealing to me than when he was saying "See ya!" and walking off with a suitcase in his hand. I've always thought that one of these days I'd like to fly off somewhere like that, with just a casual "See ya!"

I swung up from my heels on the fourteenth pitch, got under the ball, and sent it up at a good angle. Frank shouted *"No!"* and I shouted *"Go!"* but the ball ended up in the netting a good meter below the target. From there on it was all downhill. My anxiety over the prospect of losing my entire evening's wages destroyed my form, making me swing for the sky, and the best I could do on the remaining pitches was some useless grounders. When, on the seventeenth pitch, I whiffed again, I heard Frank stifle a laugh, and that made me lose my cool entirely. None of the last three balls even made it into fair territory.

"Boy, that was close! I thought I was done for, several times."

Frank was feigning sympathy for me. I felt I needed to do something. There was no way I could accept having to work for this clown for free, even for one night. I came out of the cage, and before putting my jacket back on I held the bat out to him and said: "Your turn, Frank."

Frank didn't take the bat. He played dumb and said: "Whaddaya mean?"

"Your turn to try. Same bet."

"Wait a minute, nobody said anything about that."

"You used to play baseball, right? I already hit. Now you're up."

"Like I said before, I'm tired. Much too tired to swing a bat."

I braced myself.

"You're a liar," I said.

Sure enough, this summoned up the Face. Little blue and red capillaries appeared on his cheeks, the light went out of his pupils, and the corners of his eyes and nose and lips began to quiver. This was the first time I'd seen the Face head-on and close up, so close I could almost feel Frank's breath on me. He looked like he was either very, very angry or very, very frightened.

"What are you talking about?" he said, peering at me with those lightless eyes. "I don't know what you're talking about. You're calling me a liar? Why? When have I ever lied to you?"

I looked down at my shoes. I didn't want to look at the Face. Frank seemed to be trying to arrange it into a sad, hurt expression, and it wasn't a pleasant sight. I felt pathetic just being associated with a face like that.

"You said you used to play baseball when you were little. You told me that, in the waiting room at the peep show. You said you and your brothers didn't have anything else to do so you played baseball all the time."

"So how does that make me a liar?"

"For anybody who's played it as a child, baseball is a sacred thing. Right?"

"I don't get you."

"It's sacred, more important than anything."

"Okay, Kenji, hold on a minute. I think I'm beginning to see. I guess you're saying that if what I said in the waiting room is true, then I should take a turn at the plate?"

"Exactly. Isn't that what we did as kids? We always took turns batting."

"All right," Frank said. He took the bat and stepped into the cage. "Double or nothing, then?"

The guy in the training wear was packing up to leave. Except for the dozing attendant and the bum, we were the only ones on this bizarre concrete plateau in a canyon of love hotels.

"That's right," I said. "If you hit the home run target, my fee for tomorrow night also is zero. If you don't hit it, you pay me the regular fee for both nights."

Frank nodded, but before putting the coins in the slot, he hesitated and said: "Kenji, I don't really understand how this happened. All I know is I'm stepping up to swing this bat because you're in a bad mood. But I just want us to get along. You know what I mean?"

"Yes."

"It's not like I tried to get you mad so you'd take the bet and I wouldn't have to pay you. I'm not that kind of person, Kenji. I was just playing around, feeling like a kid again. It's not about money—I've got plenty of money. I guess I don't look like a rich fellow, but that doesn't mean I'm not one. You wanna look in my wallet?"

Before I could refuse, Frank pulled a wallet from his breast pocket. A different wallet from the one he'd taken out in the lingerie pub, which had been made of imitation snakeskin. This one was of well-worn black leather, and inside was a thick wad of ¥10,000 notes and another of $100 bills. "See?" he said and smiled. What this was supposed to prove, I couldn't tell you. Genuine rich guys never carry a lot of cash around, and I didn't see any credit cards in there.

"That's about 4000 bucks and 280,000 yen. Oh, I've got money, all right. You see that now?"

"Yeah, I see," I said, and Frank strained to make the happiest face he was capable of. His cheeks twisted grotesquely, and he kept them like that until I grinned back at him. I felt goosebumps rise on the nape of my neck.

"All right, then. Here goes."

Frank took ¥300 out of his coin purse and fed the machine. Then, instead of standing on the artificial turf of the batter's box, he stepped onto the concrete and stood directly on top of the painted lines of home plate. I had no idea why he was doing that. If he didn't move before the pitch came, he was going to get hit by the ball. The green light came on, and the machine began to stir. Still standing on home plate, Frank crouched down facing the machine and held the bat out in front of his chest. His grip was wrong too—his right hand below his left. I thought he was trying to be funny. I heard the spring's final stretch and then the thump as it snapped back. Frank still wasn't moving, and the ball grazed his ear at 100 kph. Well after the ball had hit the mat behind him, he swung for all he was worth—if you can call it a swing. He pounded the bat against the concrete, as if he were chopping wood, and let out an incomprehensible yowl. The metal bat slipped out of his grasp and bounced up in the air, ringing like a high-pitched gong. When the next pitch came whizzing at him Frank was standing sideways to the ball but still right on top of home plate. I was dumbfounded. I was watching an adult American male stand in the path of a speeding baseball with nothing in his hands. That familiar, everyday concept—the batter's box—had been transformed into something alien. Frank's pose had nothing to do with baseball, or any other sport. He squatted there with his head bowed and his fists still locked in the position they were in when the bat flew off—one on top of the other, both pointing toward left field. It was as if he'd been instantaneously freeze-dried. The second ball grazed his back, and I called out to him: "Hey, Frank." He didn't even flinch. He was staring at the bluish white concrete floor. A scrap of paper rode a gust of wind through the chain-link fence and danced lazily in the air to the ancient pop song crackling over the loudspeakers. Frank wasn't even blinking. It was as if rigor mortis had set in. I felt like I'd wandered into a nightmare. One ball after another brushed past Frank and slammed against the mat suspended behind him. The regular, muffled sound it made was like the ticking of time in some alternate world—strangely comical but also painfully real. The sixth ball hit Frank in the ass, but he still didn't move except to bring his hands in front of his face and peer at them. It was a pose of sorrow and resignation, like someone who'd just confessed to a crime and was awaiting punishment. I began to feel I'd been bullying him and went into the cage to try and put a stop to it all. "This is dangerous, Frank," I said and put my hand on his shoulder, which was as cold and hard to the touch as the metal bat had been. "It's dangerous here," I said again, shaking him. Frank finally looked up from his hands and nodded. His face was turned toward me, but his dead eyes were focused somewhere else, and as I led him from the cage he slipped on a stray ball and fell down. I apologized to him again and again. I felt like I'd crossed a line, done something unforgivable.

"It's all right, Kenji," he said when he'd settled into the chair again. "I'm okay now."

"You want to go get a cup of coffee or something?" I asked.

Frank shook his head, trying to smile, and said: "Let me sit here for a while."

The homeless man was watching us.

2

December 30, 1996.

I got up around noon and read the newspaper first thing. It was full of details about the schoolgirl murder.

In the early morning hours of December 28, a restaurant employee in the Kabuki-cho section of Shinjuku, Tokyo, reported to police that on leaving work he had discovered two plastic trash bags containing the dismembered body of a young woman. Police have identified the woman as Akiko Takahashi (17), a second-year student at Taito No. 2 High School and the daughter of Nobuyuki Takahashi (48) of Taito Ward. Evidence suggests that Akiko had been sexually assaulted, and the Metropolitan Police have formed a task force to investigate the case as an apparent rape/homicide.

Investigators report that Akiko's torso was found in one bag and her head, arms, and legs in the other. Her face bore several bruises, and cuts and puncture wounds covered her body. It was determined that she had been dead for approximately twelve hours. Her clothing, appointment book, and other personal effects were also found inside the plastic bags, which were discovered at a trash collection site in an out-of-the-way alley. Because of the small amount of blood at the scene, the task force has concluded that Akiko's remains were transported there after she had been assaulted, murdered, and dismembered at a separate location.

It is known that Akiko was associated with a group of juvenile delinquents who frequented Kabuki-cho and nearby Ikebukuro. The Nishi-Shinjuku police have interviewed members of the group and learned that Akiko was last seen in the early evening hours of December 27, at an Ikebukuro game center. . . .

I had finished reading and turned on the TV when the doorbell rang. I opened up to find Jun standing there, dangling a bag from a convenience store. "It's just instant," she said, "but would you like some hot-pot noodles?"

"You really think he . . . ? What was this gaijin's name again?"

"Frank."

"Right. You really think he's the murderer?"

"I'm not saying that, but . . . I don't know."

On TV a psychologist, a criminologist, and a social commentator guy who was supposed to be an expert on high-school girls were holding forth, acting as if nothing in the whole world was beyond their comprehension.

"I mean, I don't have any actual evidence that he did it. The real mystery to me is why I can't shake the feeling that maybe he did."

The thick noodles were delicious. Jun had mixed in some minced meat she'd bought separately. She's thoughtful like that. Jun has bleached highlights in her hair and piercings in both ears. Today she'd shown up in a black leather miniskirt with a mohair-blend sweater and boots. On TV, the social commentator guy was saying: "As for the baggy leggings and the bleached hair and the piercings, these are all expressions of high-school girls' rejection of the parameters of adult society." Jun picked up a tiny clump of minced meat with her chopsticks and said the guy was a fool. I agreed with her. I'm not a girl, and it's been two years since I was in high school, so I'd never claim to understand even Jun very well. But some of the younger "experts" on TV act as if they've got high-school girls completely figured out. You can't trust people like that.

"Chopping her up, though," Jun said, "—that's pretty extreme. It's like *Silence of the Lambs*, don't you think?"

"Yeah, I do. I think whoever did it must have been influenced by stuff like that. Like you said last night, it's not a very Japanese way to kill somebody."

"So did you bring me a picture?"

"A picture?"

"Kenji, you said you'd bring a Print Club photo of the guy."

"I didn't get back here till almost three in the morning, after dropping him off at his hotel. He said something you wouldn't believe last night, at this batting center we went to. Believe me, photos were the last thing on my mind. We went to this batting center and he got all whacked out."

"What do you mean, whacked out?"

"He suddenly froze up, his whole body. The balls were flying at him and he was facing the wrong way, just squatting there like a statue. It wasn't just, you know, like he'd never played baseball before or something. It was way beyond that. And when I asked him about it afterward, he told me he's missing part of his brain."

"You mean, like a retard or something?"

"No. They cut it out. Part of his brain."

The noodles Jun was lifting to her mouth stopped and swayed in midair.

"Don't you die if somebody cuts out part of your brain?"

"This was the part called the . . . what was it again? I asked Frank to spell it for me and looked it up, and it was a word you hear once in a while. What the hell was it? Can you name any parts of the brain?"

"The skull?"

"That's the bone, dummy. Anyway, it's a more difficult word."

"Medulla oblongata!"

"Not *that* difficult. It was up here in front."

An older guy, a sociologist, was now talking on the tube: "In other words, as a result of this incident, we're likely to see harsher enforcement of the anti-prostitution laws, but this, while it may have some temporary effect, would represent a total capitulation of mature judgment."

"The frontal lobe?" said Jun.

I patted her on the head. Jun's just an average student, but I think she's smarter than most. Right now her mother was on a trip to Saipan that she'd won in some kind of lottery, which meant that Jun could have slept over last night without getting busted, but she has a brother in middle school, for one thing, so she'd gone home around midnight, as usual. It's not that she's the serious, responsible type—Jun's goal is to avoid extremes like that and be as normal as possible. It isn't easy to live a normal life, though. Parents, teachers, government—they all teach you how to live the dreary, deadening life of a slave, but nobody teaches you how to live normally.

"That's it, the frontal lobe, and there was something else but it was more difficult and not in the dictionary. Anyway, they cut it out. His frontal lobe."

"Why?"

"What?"

"Why did they cut it out? Isn't it something you need?"

"He says he was in a car accident, and his skull got cracked open and little bits of glass got in there, so they had to remove it. Sounds ridiculous, right? But if you had seen him last night..."

Frank had said: "Kenji, can I tell you a secret?" And before I could even reply, he was off. "It may have crossed your mind that there's something unusual about me. Well, when I was eleven I was in a terrible automobile accident, and it damaged my brain, so sometimes, like just now, I suddenly can't move my body, or my speech comes out all mangled and nobody can understand what I'm saying, or I'll blurt out things that seem completely unconnected."

Frank took my hand and placed it on the back of his wrist and said: See how cold this is? He wasn't kidding. It was freezing out there, with a strong wind whipping through the open concrete platform. I had the sniffles, and my own hands were half-numb. But the cold of Frank's wrist was a different sort of cold, a cold you couldn't have fixed by rubbing it or something. His wrist and forearm felt just like his shoulder had when I was dragging him out of the batting cage, like something metallic. Once when I was small I went with my father to a warehouse where they kept the machines he designed. I forget exactly why he took me with him, but it was in the hills outside Nagoya, in the middle of winter. Rows and rows of giant machines whose functions were a complete mystery to me, all lined up in this vast space charged with the smell of chilled steel. Touching Frank's wrist triggered that memory.

"Yet I myself can't even feel how cold my body is," he told me. "I've lost some of my sensory functions, and a lot of times I get so I can't even tell if this body is really mine or not. Or I can be talking away like this and suddenly my memory will get very uncertain, and I won't know if what I'm saying really happened or if it's all just something I dreamed."

Frank went on about this all the way back to his hotel. It seemed like something from a science fiction movie, but I decided to take it at face value. Not so much because it explained the things he said and did, but because of the way his arm and shoulder felt to the touch.

"I don't get it," Jun said. She had finished her noodles. I still had more than half of mine left. I have a sensitive tongue, and steaming-hot boiled *udon* takes me some time. "You're not saying he's a robot, are you?"

"Well, I mean, look, all we know about robots is what we see in comics or movies or whatever, but . . . It's like, there's a certain sensation you get from touching someone's skin, right?"

I put my hand on the back of Jun's. We hadn't had sex for a while—almost three weeks, now that I thought about it. When we first met we were going at it like a couple of I-don't-know-what in heat, but gradually, as we spent more time hanging out with each other, eating noodles or Jun's special salads, the sex became less frequent.

"It's a particular kind of soft, warm feeling that you recognize immediately. Well, when you touch Frank it's not like that at all."

Jun's eyes were on the TV, but she squeezed my hand gently and told me to hurry up and finish eating.

"Before the stuff they're saying ruins your appetite."

They were still going on about the schoolgirl murder. The experts had all had their say, and now a reporter was chattering excitedly in front of a big, badly drawn sketch of a generic high-school girl: "Akiko had been viciously beaten, but if you'll look at this picture I'd like to explain some of the more puzzling facts in regard to the nature of her injuries. . . ."

"Don't these people ever think about how her parents would feel if they saw this?" Jun said. "They act like the girls who sell it aren't even human."

Makes me sick, she muttered, looking away from the TV. It's true the drawing was in incredibly bad taste. There were different-colored marks for where the girl's body was bruised, slashed, or punctured, and the head and arms and legs were separated from the torso with dotted lines. "So, as you can see, Akiko's entire body had wounds of one sort or another, and on her upper torso, right here, on her left breast, the flesh was said to have been sliced and peeled away, but to the profiling experts the most significant point is here, the eyes, the fact that her eyes had been punctured with what would appear to be an ice pick, which, according to criminal psychologists, means that the murderer couldn't bear to have the act witnessed, that he didn't want the victim watching him and found it necessary to blind her before proceeding with the attack, and what's important about this is that it tells us the murderer is an extremely repressed and timid person."

"Maybe not, though," said Jun. "Maybe he just likes to puncture people's eyeballs."

I thought so too. On the screen, we were getting closeups of the housewives in the audience and the regular "personalities" on the panel. Their reactions ranged from disgust and disbelief to defiant outrage. The reporter continued: "Akiko, it has become clear, was part of a group involved in underage prostitution, and police are doing their best to determine the identities of her most recent clients. However, if a girl is plying this dubious trade independently, as opposed to being affiliated with one of the notorious 'date clubs,' tracing previous clients can prove almost impossible."

"They could check her pager," Jun said. "I'm sure she had one, and if it was still on her, they could trace her last ten messages—or is it twenty?—through the phone company."

"I don't think the paper said anything about a pager, either, now that you mention it."

"They probably aren't telling us everything, because the murderer would be reading the paper and watching TV, and if he realized they had any leads he'd leave the country or something. I would if I were him."

The reporter finished his bit, and now it was back to the experts and the minor showbiz personalities on the panel. One of these was saying something that was definitely slanted against the victim: "With all due respect to the young lady who was murdered, we're only going to see more cases of a similar nature as long as this so-called compensated dating is allowed to continue among high-school girls, because although generally speaking these girls are just spoiled, selfish children, physically they're adults, and I warn you that there's no telling how bad things could get if we don't clamp down and punish them accordingly, and of course I'm referring to the men who patronize these girls as well, they too are responsible for this state of affairs, and we need to let them know that they can and will be arrested, because if we let something like this go, if we turn a blind eye and don't take action now, the next thing you know we truly will be like America—a society in chaos!"

The audience of housewives burst into applause.

"They don't have compensated dating in America," Jun said. "I wonder what these geniuses would say if an American newspaper asked them to explain *why* Japanese high-school girls sell it."

The word "America" brought me back to Frank. When we'd reached his hotel, he turned to me to say one last thing.

"I've been told I'm a very unusual case," he said. "Normally you stop making new brain cells after a certain age, whereas the liver for example—or was it the stomach?—one of them makes millions of new cells every day, same with the skin, but the brain, after you've reached adulthood, all it does is lose cells. My doctor, however, says that in my case the brain may be creating new cells to replace the part that was cut out, which would mean that inside my head I have old cells and new ones mixing together. I think that's why my memory gets so hazy sometimes, and my motor functions get all fouled up. I mean, that could explain it, don't you think, Kenji?"

On TV they took a break from the schoolgirl murder and moved on to some news flashes. The first headline nearly made me spit out my last mouthful of noodles: HOMELESS MAN FOUND TORCHED TO DEATH.

"In other news, an unidentified body, burned beyond recognition, was found in a pay toilet in Shinjuku Central Park this morning. Discovered by city sanitation workers, the victim appeared to have been doused with a flammable substance and set on fire. The intensity of the fire was such that the concrete inner walls of the restroom were scorched and blackened, according to police. They are investigating the incident as a possible homicide. From the victim's presumed belongings, which were piled in old shopping bags outside the restroom, he is believed to have been one of the homeless men who inhabit the park. Next, reporting from just outside the Japanese embassy in Lima, Peru, where the hostage crisis continues..."

The noodles in my mouth had turned to yarn. It was as if Frank's face had suddenly loomed up before my eyes.

"What's wrong?" Jun leaned forward and peered at me.

I swallowed with effort, then stood up, got a bottle of mineral water from the fridge, and took a drink. I felt sick to my stomach.

"You're all pale."

Jun came over next to me and rubbed my back. I could feel her soft, girlish hand through my sweater. Imagine, I thought. Imagine not even being able to feel something like this.

"That gaijin again?"

"His name's Frank."

"Right. Frank. It's so common it's hard to remember."

"Yeah, well, it may not even be his real name."

"You think it's a whatchamacallit? An alias?"

I told her all the things Frank had said about homeless people the night before.

"But, wait a minute," Jun said when I was done. "If the gaijin—sorry—if Frank says there might be people who would see a smelly homeless man and want to cuddle up to him but look at a baby and want to kill it . . ."

"When it comes to this guy, it's not about making sense. I get the feeling you can't believe anything he says anyway—except for the hateful stuff."

"So you think he killed the homeless man?"

It was hard to explain why, exactly. I had no proof, and Jun had never met Frank. You couldn't understand what was so disturbing about him without meeting him.

"Kenji, why not cancel the job?"

Cancel on Frank? The thought literally gave me goosebumps.

"I can't do that," I said.

"Why? You think he might kill you?"

Jun was really beginning to worry. She could sense how scared I was. She probably pictured Frank as the sort of psychopath Mafia killer you see in movies. But Frank was no hit man. Hit men murder people for a fee. If Frank was a murderer, I was pretty sure he wasn't just in it for the money.

"I doubt if I can explain this very well. I can't prove he's done anything, and normally it wouldn't even occur to me that he might have. The homeless guy who got killed—I don't know that he's the same guy we saw at the batting center. And I don't see any point in going back there to check, because I have a feeling that to somebody like Frank, one bum would be as good as another."

"I'm not really following you."

"I know," I sighed. "I think I'm starting to lose it."

"Did the homeless man at the batting center do something to Frank?"

"Nothing, no."

"So what exactly makes you think Frank had something to do with killing him?"

"It's crazy, I know. I'm sure it's just paranoia. But if you were to meet him . . . You said you wanted to see a photo of him, but I don't think a photo would tell you that much. How can I put this? Listen, when I was in high school, we had a lot of badasses around—you probably do too, right? In your school? Kids who seem to go out of their way to cause trouble and make people hate them?"

"I don't know. Nobody that bad, I don't think."

Probably not, now that she mentioned it. Jun goes to a fairly respectable private high for girls, where there probably aren't many really hard cases. Or, then again, maybe the type who gets off on being a big pain in the ass for everyone else is slowly dying out.

"Well, anyway, that's the sort of negative energy I sense about Frank, only taken to the ultimate extreme. The ultimate in malevolence."

"Malevolence."

"Yeah. Everybody has a little of that in them. I know I do, and to some extent even . . . Well, maybe not you, Jun. You're too sweet."

"Never mind about me. Try to explain this better. You're the one who's so good at explaining things."

"Okay. Look. I had a friend who was like that—hated by everybody. The teachers had long since given up on him, and he ended up stabbing the headmaster with an X-Acto knife and getting expelled. But, see, he had a very troubled home life, this guy, not that he talked about it much, but once I went to his house. His mother gave me this super-polite welcome, bowing and everything, and the house, the house was huge and the guy had his own room, way bigger than anything I ever had, and all the latest computer stuff, everything you could think of, and I remember being really envious, except that something was weird about the atmosphere of the place. I couldn't say exactly what, but something was weird about it. So his mother brings us tea and cookies and says something like 'Our son's told us so much about you' or whatever, and my friend goes, 'Never mind that, get the hell out of here,' and she's like 'Well, please do make yourself at home' and leaves the room bowing again. I'm like, 'Thanks,' you know, watching her close the door, and my friend looks at me and goes, 'Bitch used to whip me with a hose.' No particular expression on his face or anything, just 'You know those extension pipes on vacuum cleaners? She used to hit me with one' and 'Burned me with a lighter too.' He showed me the burn scars on his arms, and he goes, 'I've got a little brother, but she never laid a finger on him.' So, anyway, later on we started playing this computer game that'd just come out, and after a while I had to go to the bathroom, so we pause the game and I go out into the hallway, and his mother is standing there in the shadows. She's staring at me with this spaced-out look on her face and then suddenly she goes, 'Oh, the lavatory? It's down at the end,' or whatever, and titters in this high-pitched voice, a voice like, I don't know how to describe it, like a needle hitting a nerve. . . . This friend, say we'd go to a game center or something? And if there'd be some friction with dudes from another school, if one of them said something—I mean anything at all, any little thing, like, Come on, you've been on that machine for two hours, let somebody else have a turn—my friend's face would undergo this transformation. He'd get this look like, you know, there's no telling what the son of a bitch might do. Like he was no longer in control of himself. Well, Frank has that same face times ten. Like he's just completely gone."

"A scary face, in other words," Jun said.

"Yeah, but not like a yakuza scowling at you or something, not scary in that way," I told her, thinking: Sure enough, it's hard to explain. I imagine other people could meet Frank and not get this feeling from him at all. If he happened to stop you on the street and hold out a camera and ask you to take a photo for him, say, you might come away thinking he seemed nice—kind of down on his luck, maybe, but a well-meaning, open and friendly gaijin.

"Forget it. I can't explain. Anyway he's a really weird guy, but 'anyway he's a really weird guy' doesn't tell you much, does it?"

"No, it doesn't. Besides, if you think about it, Kenji, I've never spent any time with foreigners, like you have. That must make a difference. I mean, how could you know what's weird about one unless you know lots of them?"

What Jun said made sense. The Japanese aren't exactly in tune with people from other countries. My last client, or rather the one before last, a man from Texas, had told me how astonished he was when he went to Shibuya. He said: "I thought I was in Harlem or someplace, all those kids walking around looking like black hip-hop artists, wearing their Walkmans, some had skateboards, too, but what was amazing was, here they are completely copying the fashions of African-American kids—even down to the dark suntans and cornrows—and they can't speak a word of English! But I guess they just like black people, huh?" I don't know what to do with questions like that. There's no way to answer them. I told the Texan something like, Well, they think imitating black people is cool—but even I knew it wasn't much of an answer. There are things people in this country do automatically that foreigners can't understand no matter how hard you try to explain.

"Why don't we go for a walk?" Jun said.

It seemed like a good idea.

As we were leaving my apartment, Jun found something stuck to the outside of my door and said: "What's this?" It was a small, dark thing, about half the size of a postage stamp, like a torn scrap of paper. My first thought was that it was a piece of human skin. "Kenji, what is it?" she asked again.

"I don't know," I said, picking at it with my thumb and forefinger. "The wind must have blown it against the door."

Touching it gave me the creeps, and it was fastened to the metal door as if with glue. I had to scrape it off with my fingernail, leaving a dark stain on the door. I tossed it away, into the bushes beyond the stairs. My heart was pounding like crazy. I felt ill but tried not to let on.

"I wonder if it was there when I came," Jun said as we walked down the stairs. "I didn't notice it."

I was convinced it was human skin. And that Frank had put it there. Whose skin, I couldn't say. The schoolgirl's? The homeless guy's? Or maybe he'd sliced it off some corpse that hadn't been discovered yet. My head was reeling, and I felt sick to my stomach.

Jun stopped at the bottom of the stairs. "You've gone all pale again, Kenji."

I knew I should say something, but no words came.

"Let's go back to the room," she said. "The wind's too cold out here anyway."

If it was human skin, and Frank had put it there, why did I throw it away? Because I couldn't bear the feel of it for even a split second.

"Kenji, come on, let's go back in." Jun was patting my arm.

"No," I said. "No, let's walk."

I kept imagining Frank lurking somewhere, watching us walking along arm in arm. Jun peered up at my face from time to time but didn't talk. The thing had had what felt like fingerprint grooves pressed into it. It wasn't a scrap of paper, I was sure of that. And I couldn't imagine that this damp little thing, about the size of a fingernail, had just happened to come wafting along on the wind to plaster itself to my door. Someone had deliberately pasted it there, pushing down hard with the tip of his finger.

It must be a warning, I thought. And the only person I knew who might feel any need to warn me would be Frank. Don't get any ideas or try anything funny, or you could end up like this, was probably what it meant. An image flashed through my mind of Frank planting that moist scrap of skin on my door and muttering: "Kenji, you'll understand what this means, won't you." It was behavior that suited him perfectly.

My friends have always told me I'm a pessimist, that I tend to see the dark side of everything, and I think that may have something to do with Dad dying when I was so young. It was definitely a shock when he died. The worst possible scenario is always taking shape behind the scenes, where no one can detect it or see it coming, and then one day, *boom,* it becomes your reality. And once it's real, it's too late to do anything about it. That's what I learned from my father's death.

Jun and I neared Meguro Station, walking among the crowds. She could see I wasn't quite myself and didn't press me to talk. Jun's parents divorced when she was small, so she knows what it's like to be anxious or scared and want to be with somebody but not have to talk. I think people like Jun and me are becoming the mainstream in this country. Very few people of our generation or the next will reach adulthood without experiencing the sort of unhappiness you can't really deal with on your own. We're still in the minority, so the media lump us together as "The Oversensitive Young," or whatever the latest catchphrase is, but eventually that will change.

I tried calling the office of the magazine where I advertise my services. Maybe Frank had asked for my address.

"Yokoyama-san?"

"Kenji! You still working?"

Yokoyama-san published the magazine more or less on his own, and though it was the day before New Year's Eve, he was hard at it now. In fact he often sleeps in his office and works most Sundays and national holidays. He always says he's happiest when he's listening to old-time jazz and laying out the magazine on his Mac.

"Yes, I am," I said. "Gaijin don't think of New Year's the way we do, as you know."

"And that's all to their credit if you ask me. Hey—did the police contact you?"

My heart stopped for a second. It turned out not to be about Frank, though.

"Did something happen?"

"You knew I had a homepage, right? On the internet?"

"Of course. You're always bragging about having designed it yourself."

"I am? Well, anyway, the police sent me a warning."

"A warning? What for?"

"I had a few pictures on there. Nothing hardcore, but nudes, of course. After all, it's a magazine for foreigners about the Japanese sex industry. But the police advised me to 'practice self-restraint.' In other words, clean it up or expect some heat. Hey, you could see some pubic hair, it's true, but every magazine you pick up these days shows at least that much, so it's obvious they just want to make an example of me. I was afraid since your ad's in there they might have contacted you too."

"They haven't."

"Good. If they do call you, just say you don't know anything."

"I will. By the way," I said, "you didn't get any calls from a client of mine, did you?"

Even if Frank had called, I was pretty sure Yokoyama-san wouldn't have given him my address.

"Oh yeah, I did," he said.

My heart started thumping. I was using my mobile, standing beneath the sign of a cake shop near Meguro Station with my back to the wind. Jun was holding my hand and watching a live demonstration in the shop window of how to decorate a cake Japanese New Year–style. Every now and then she shot me a worried look.

"You did? Who was it?"

"What did he say his name was again? John, James, one of those names you hear all the time. He wanted your bank account number. I didn't give it to him, of course, but . . . It was a pretty strange call, now that you mention it."

"Strange? In what way? Was he calling from here in Tokyo?"

"That's the thing, he said he was calling from . . . where was it, Missouri? Kansas, maybe. Anyway, somewhere in America. He calls me last night in the middle of the night. Closer to dawn, really. Pretty inconsiderate of the guy, I thought, or just plain ignorant. I'm sure he said one of those Midwestern states, so do the math—over there it's December 29, Sunday afternoon. Who's going to call from America on Sunday afternoon to ask me for your account number? Strange, right? Over there they all go to church on Sunday, don't they? Or to the movies or whatever, but who'd make an international call to say I forgot to pay my guide, give me his bank account number? If it was the other way around I'd understand, if he was saying you owed *him* money, I could see that—but to tell me he wants to pay *you*? Besides, you're the one he should be calling, right? So I asked him, I said, 'Did you call Kenji?'"

"And?"

"He said you didn't answer. Any idea who it was?"

"Well, for starters, I always insist on cash or traveler's checks. I'm not about to trust people to wire me my fee from overseas."

"Of course not. Ask any hustler her golden rule—it's got to be cash on the—Wait, that didn't sound right. I'm not saying you're—"

"What was he like? His voice and everything."

"His voice. Well, the first thing that seemed odd to me was that he sounded so close. I know the international lines are pretty good these days, but still, there was no static or delay or anything. . . . His voice? I don't really remember. It was the type you don't remember, a voice you might hear anywhere, not husky or deep or high-pitched or anything. Pretty average way of speaking too. Not the most beautiful English but polite enough. That's about all I can tell you. Is there a problem?"

"Not really." I knew better than to think I could explain.

"The last thing he said was really strange, something about magic."

I wasn't sure I'd heard this right.

"Sorry?"

"I think he realized I was getting suspicious. This was the middle of the night, after all. I mean, look, I'm a man who likes foreigners. Normally I'd bend over backward to help, but to have this guy wake me up before dawn and mutter this crazy stuff in my ear, I mean, come on. I may have been a little gruff when I said did you call Kenji, but then he starts telling me what a great guy you were and what a wonderful job you did, and how well he and you got along and how you hung out together like friends, and I just thought, this is getting weirder and weirder. I mean, would an American telephone somebody he's never met from his living room or whatever in Kansas or Missouri on Sunday afternoon to say that the tour guide who introduced him to women at sex clubs in Tokyo was a great guy? Normally, I mean."

I had a vision of Frank, his scrap of human flesh at the ready, calling

Yokoyama-san from his hotel room before dawn and saying: Kenji was a wonderful fellow, please tell me his bank account number. That was exactly the sort of bizarre behavior he was made for. As opposed to, say, giving himself a Mohawk, painting his body, and running naked through the streets.

"How do you know it was Frank?" Jun asked me. We were sitting at a table in the little "Café Corner" of the cake shop. After talking to Yokoyama-san I'd been standing there on the sidewalk stunned till she grabbed my arm and dragged me inside, saying I was pale as a ghost, let's get some hot coffee. We both had cappuccinos, which were supposed to be special in this place, but I couldn't taste mine. It was as if I had some sort of film covering my tongue and gums and throat. My heart was pounding and my mind was confused. I told her what Yokoyama-san had said.

"Of course, there's no proof it was Frank," I added unconvincingly.

"You think he stuck that thing on your door, too, don't you?"

Sort of, I said. I hadn't told her what I thought the "thing" was. Jun was too important to me. I didn't want to share with her something as insane and intense and evil as what I was imagining. I wanted to handle it on my own, if possible. Spilling my guts to her about this would do nothing to brighten her life, that was for sure. But I should have known there was no way to hide anything from a sixteen-year-old girl. Sixteen-year-old girls are probably the most sensitive and perceptive group of people in this entire country.

"That thing was funny," Jun said in an oddly childlike tone of voice. Like a nursery school kid seeing a corpse on the steps and telling her teacher: There's a man sleeping outside!

"It looked like papyrus, didn't it?" she said.

"Ah. 'The fruit that tastes like first love,' as they say in the ads?"

"Kenji."

"What?"

"Normally I like your little puns, but now's not the time."

I hadn't meant it as a joke. I'd honestly mistaken "papyrus" for "papaya." I'm not proud to admit it, but that's how out of it I was.

"Did it have blood on it or something, that thing? It was all dark and nasty-looking. Was that blood?"

"I think so," I confessed, throwing in the sponge. I didn't have the energy left to lie. "I think it was a piece of someone's skin."

"What? Why would he do that?"

"As a warning. Warning me not to talk to the police or whatever."

My mobile rang in my jacket pocket. Dark forebodings always come true. It was Frank.

"Hi, Kenji!" in this super-cheerful voice. "How you feeling?"

He seemed to be at a pay phone, and it sounded like the words were coming not out of his mouth but straight through his skull from his brain. On our table was a little clipboard with a sign: *Please refrain from using your mobile phone in the Café Corner.* Jun pointed at it and gestured that I should go outside, but a cute young waitress who'd been rearranging cakes in the window said it was all right, since there weren't any other customers right now. Jun thanked her. This little cake shop was a favorite of Jun's, and apparently she and the waitress had struck up an acquaintance. It was unnerving to hear Frank talk as I watched Jun and the waitress interacting. His voice had the power to transform an everyday little scene like this into something else entirely. I felt like I was being sucked through the gap between what Frank's voice symbolized and what Jun and the waitress symbolized, down into the belly of some monster.

"I'm fine," I told him, struggling to keep my voice calm. Don't let on, I told myself. Act like you know nothing. Let him think you're just some dim-witted nightlife guide.

"Good! So I'll see you tonight?"

"Nine o'clock?" I said.

"More fun—I can't wait! Last night was fantastic!"

"I'm glad you enjoyed it."

"Oh, and by the way, I changed hotels."

My pulse was racing again, and my throat was bone dry.

"Oh? Which hotel?"

"One of those highrise places by the new government buildings. The Hilton."

"And your room number?"

"I wanted to switch to a nicer hotel since I'm only going to be here two more nights, but it was hard to find a room, what with New Year's and all. They tell me that in Japan New Year's Day is like our Christmas."

He didn't give me a room number. I doubted he was staying at the Hilton. What he was really telling me was that I couldn't find him even if I tried.

"How's your girlfriend?"

I wondered if he was watching us right now, and scanned the street outside the window.

"Oh, she's fine. I'm surprised you remember I've got one."

"I was afraid she might be mad because I kept you out later than planned last night. She wasn't, was she? Girls—you know how selfish they can be."

Was he watching us right now? Did he know I was with Jun?

"She wasn't mad. Actually I'm with her now. Everything is fine."

"You're on a date? Oh, heck, I'm sorry to bother you!"

"No, it's all right, I'm glad you called. You didn't look well when I left you last night. I was worried."

"I'm okay now, and I'm really sorry for all the trouble I caused you. Today it feels like my brain is regenerating like crazy. I can tell a whole lot of new brain cells are being produced, and I can't wait till tonight, tonight I want to have sex for sure!"

"Frank, could you tell me your room number at the Hilton? In case there's an emergency and I need to get in touch with you?"

"What do you mean, emergency? Like what?"

"I don't know, nothing major, but if there's a mix-up on where to meet or if something happens and I'm going to be late, wouldn't it be better if I had your—"

"Oh. Right. Well, actually I haven't checked in yet. I made a reservation and left my luggage there, but the room's not ready."

"Will you call me again when you know the number, then?"

"Of course. Oh but wait, I'll probably be out all day and might not have a chance to call. And if I'm out you wouldn't be able to get me anyway."

"Do you mind if I ask the front desk?"

"Um, I'm afraid that's no good, I'm staying under a different name—I mean, not Frank. You know how it is. I plan to have some fun the next couple of nights—naughty fun, if you know what I mean—so I didn't want to use my real name. But as for where to meet tonight, how about out in front of the batting center?"

"I'm sorry, what did you just say?"

"Out in front of the batting center we went to last night. The batting cages were on the second floor, right? Not there but at street level, remember the game center? Right around there. I liked that place."

"Frank, I've never arranged to meet anybody in a spot like that before. I prefer to go to the client's hotel. Why don't we meet in the lobby of the Hilton?"

"Well, I was there earlier, and it's not really my kind of place. I don't feel at ease there. What can I say? It's so crowded and noisy and kind of snobbish, don't you think? I don't like it there so much. I'm a country boy originally, you know, and I just can't relax in a place like that."

So why did he change hotels? A minute ago he'd told me he wanted to move to a nicer place because he only had two nights left.

"Frank, I'm coming down with a bit of a cold. I don't want to be outside any more than I have to. Can't we meet somewhere inside a building? Besides—" I was going to add that a lot of dangerous characters hang out in that area, but he interrupted me.

"All right, of course, you're right, it's stupid to meet outside, what the hell was I thinking? I'm sorry, Kenji, but, you know, I really had fun yesterday. I had a little episode at the end there, but I'll never forget how nice you were to me. That batting center will always be one of my best memories, I just want you to know that. But never mind, let's meet somewhere else, but not the lobby of the Hilton."

"How about your hotel from last night, the Shinjuku Prince? It's near Kabuki-cho. Or would you rather check out some other—"

"No problem," Frank said. "I love that place."

"All right. I'll see you at nine o'clock in the same cafeteria off the lobby."

I was about to hang up when Frank said something that stopped me again.

"Kenji, why don't you bring your girlfriend?"

"*What*?" I said a little too loudly and looked up at Jun's face. She was still stirring her cappuccino—hadn't even taken a sip yet—and watching me with a worried look.

"Maybe I misunderstood you just now, Frank. Did you say why don't I bring my girlfriend?"

"Yeah, that's what I said. I was thinking the three of us could hang out together. Is it a bad idea?"

Asking your nightlife guide to bring his girlfriend with him—it's just plain unthinkable. Did he imagine I'd already told Jun too much? Maybe he wanted to murder her outside the batting center.

"It's out of the question, Frank."

"Well, suit yourself," he said and hung up abruptly.

I took a sip of my cappuccino before giving Jun a recap of the conversation. I had to be careful to reconstruct it accurately. What Frank had said, particularly the part about changing hotels, was full of contradictions, so I knew I'd have to put everything in the right order or it wouldn't make any sense at all. I wanted to explain it to her properly. She was the only one besides me who knew how freaky he was.

When I was done, she said: "How suspicious can you get! Why don't you go to the police?"

"And tell them what?"

Jun sighed. The cappuccino was cold, and all the froth was gone, leaving it a light brown color like muddy water.

"That's true. You can hardly say you know who murdered the schoolgirl and the homeless man but don't have any proof. . . . And obviously you can't just tell them you know this gaijin named Frank who's a liar and a weirdo, but . . . How about telephoning them instead of going in person?"

"I don't know where the bastard is, and I'm sure his name isn't Frank, either—it's all lies. The cops couldn't find him if they wanted to. Now that I think about it he may not even have stayed in that hotel last night. I never actually escorted him to his room, or even saw him get his key at the front desk, and I never called him there."

"I wonder why he wanted to meet me?"

"I don't know."

"Kenji, just don't show up tonight."

"I thought about that, but . . . He hasn't paid me yet, and—"

"Who cares about the money?"

"Yeah. The truth is it's not the money, it's that I'm sure he knows where I live and there's no telling what he'll do. I'm afraid of him, Jun, that's the honest truth, okay? I'm scared shitless of Frank. I think maybe he wanted me to bring you so he could, you know, find out how much I'd told you about him."

I wasn't about to say "kill you."

A woman and her little boy and girl came into the shop. The woman was in her thirties, I'd say, the kids in elementary school. They were having a good time deciding which kind of cake they wanted. The kids were well behaved but gleeful, full of life. The mother was wearing a tasteful suit under a tasteful coat, and her interaction with the waitress was natural and courteous. When Jun turned to look their way, her eyes met the little girl's, and the little girl beamed at her. There was a time, not so long ago, when I would have looked on this sort of scene with cynicism, if not loathing. I'm not so innocent. I know what malevolence is about, which is why I thought I was able to judge that Frank was a dangerous man. Malevolence is born of negative feelings like loneliness and sadness and anger. It comes from an emptiness inside you that feels as if it's been carved out with a knife, an emptiness you're left with when something very important has been taken away from you. I can't say I sensed a particularly cruel or sadistic tendency in Frank, or even that he fit my image of a murderer. But what I did sense was an emptiness like a black hole inside him, and there was no predicting what might emerge from a place like that. I'm sure we've all experienced really malevolent feelings once or twice in our lives, the desire to kill somebody, say. But there's always a braking mechanism somewhere along the line that stops us. The malevolence is turned back, and it sinks down to the bottom of the emptiness it emerged from and lies there, forgotten, only to leak out in other ways—a passion for work, for example. Frank wasn't like that. I didn't know if he was a murderer, but I knew he had a bottomless void inside him. And that void was what made him lie. I've been there. Compared to where Frank was at, it may have been like a Hello Kitty version, but I've been there.

"Call me every half-hour," Jun said, and I nodded. "And whatever you do, don't let him get you alone."

Frank was standing in the shadow of a pillar in the lobby of the Shinjuku Prince. I was passing by on my way to the cafeteria when he popped out from behind the pillar.

"Hey, Kenji," he said.

It literally took my breath away. "Frank," I gasped. "I thought we were going to meet in the cafeteria."

It was kind of crowded, he said and winked. The world's weirdest wink: his eye rolled back in his head as he closed it, so that for a second all you could see was white. And the cafeteria, clearly visible from where we stood, was almost empty. Frank saw me looking that way and said it was really crowded a few minutes ago. He was dressed differently tonight—black sweater and corduroy jacket with jeans and sneakers. Even his hairstyle was different. The short, slicked-down bangs he'd had the night before were now standing straight up. And instead of the old leather shoulder bag, he was carrying a cloth rucksack. It was like he'd had a makeover or something.

"I found a good bar," he said, "a shot bar. You don't see many of those in this country. Let's go there first."

The bar, on Kuyakusho Avenue, is a pretty well known place. Not because it serves delicious cocktails or the interior is anything special or the food is particularly good, but simply because it's one of the few no-frills drinking places in Kabuki-cho. It's popular with foreigners, and I've taken clients there several times. It has no chairs, just a long bar and a few elbow-high tables along the big plate-glass window. To get there from the hotel we'd walked along a street lined with clubs and crowded with touts, but Frank wasn't interested in their lingerie pubs or peep shows.

"I just wanted to start off by wetting the old whistle," he said when our beers came and we clinked glasses. We could have drunk beer in the hotel cafeteria. Did Frank have some reason for not wanting to go in there? I remembered reading in a hard-boiled detective novel that if you drink in the same place two nights in a row, the bartender and waiters will remember your face.

I looked around for someone I knew. Jun had told me not to be alone with Frank, and I thought it might be a good idea to let someone who knew me see us together. Frank peered steadily at my face while he drank his beer, as if trying to read my mind. I didn't see anyone I knew. A wide range of types stood shoulder to shoulder at the bar. Affluent college kids, white-collar workers bold enough to wear suits that weren't gray or navy blue, office girls who were old hands at partying, and trendy dudes who looked like they belonged in Roppongi but had decided to drink in Kabuki-cho for a change. Later on, hostesses and girls from the sex clubs would stop in for a drink.

"You seem a bit funny somehow tonight," Frank said. He was gulping his beer at a much faster pace than he had the night before.

"I'm kind of tired," I told him. "And like I said on the phone, I think I'm catching a cold."

I guess anyone who knew me could have seen I was a bit funny somehow.

Even I thought I was. This is how people start the slide down into madness, I thought. Suspicious minds breed demons, they say, and now I knew what they meant. Frank kept peering at me, and I searched for something to say. I was trying to decide how much I should let him suspect I suspected. It seemed best to hint that I thought he was a dubious character, but not to the extent that I'd ever imagine he might be a murderer. If he knew I imagined any such thing, I was pretty sure he'd kill me. And if, on the other hand, he decided I was completely naïve and oblivious, he might be tempted to whack me just for the hell of it.

"So, what do you want to do tonight?" I asked him.

"Don't you have any good ideas, Kenji?"

In as lighthearted a tone as I could muster, I tested him with one of the cracks I'd been considering.

"Let's see. . . . Why don't we go to the batting center and hit balls till about five o'clock in the morning?"

"Five? In the morning?" he said with a smile, and when I nodded yes, yes, he laughed out loud in a very American way, raising his beer mug with one hand and slapping my shoulder with the other. An American holding a beer aloft and roaring with laughter looks as natural as a Japanese does dangling a camera and bowing. Some of the customers around us smiled. Japanese always have a favorable impression of people from overseas who seem to be having a good time. The foreigner's enjoying himself, so maybe old Nippon isn't so bad after all, in fact maybe this is a world-class bar, and we drink in places like this all the time, so maybe we're happier than we realized, is how the reasoning goes. This spot had some excellent jazz on the sound system—a rarity for Kabuki-cho—and the lighting was fashionably dim, so that not even the people standing right next to us could see Frank's face very clearly. Even as he slapped my shoulder and laughed, Frank's eyes were as cold as dark marbles. I had to force myself to return the gaze of those chilling eyes and try to look perky and cheerful. It was agony of a sort I'd never experienced before. I didn't know how long my nerves would hold up.

"I want sex, Kenji, sex. I want to drink some beer here to get in a good mood and then go to a club where I can get sexually aroused."

I had no way of knowing if my crack about the batting center had made any impression or not. In my jacket pocket was a little spray-can of mace. I'd stopped in Shibuya to buy it after parting company with Jun. Jun had suggested a stun gun, but I was afraid that if worse came to worst, I could be wiped out before getting the damn thing switched on, and keeping it switched on would drain the battery. Stun guns might be useful for attacking people, but they're not that well suited for self-defense. The safest thing would be just to get away from Frank, of course. Find him a Latin American streetwalker or a hostess from a Chinese club and send them off to a love hotel for a few hours.

"You want to buy a woman?" I asked.

"Bingo," he said. "But it's too early yet."

"There may not be many hookers out tonight, though, just two days before New Year's. Most Japanese companies are already on holiday and the businessmen have gone home. The hookers may have decided to take some time off too."

"Don't worry about that. I've done my research."

"Your what?"

"Research. After dinner I took a walk, and I questioned some fellows who were handing out fliers. You remember last night, those black fellows handing out fliers? They gave me a lot of ideas, and then I asked this woman who was standing around on the street who didn't speak much English, and she said most of the girls were working tonight. She said they came to Japan to make money, not celebrate New Year's."

"You did that all on your own, Frank? Maybe you don't need me."

How wonderful it would be, I thought, if he decided he didn't need my services and went off on his own to find a woman.

"Don't be silly, Kenji. You're more than just a guide to me now, you're my friend. You're not offended that I checked things out on my own, are you? I didn't mean to hurt your feelings or anything. Are you upset with me?"

No, no, not at all, I told him, forcing a smile. Frank was definitely different tonight. His voice was louder and more confident, and he came across as outgoing and energetic. Raring to go.

"You seem in good spirits this evening," I said. "Did you sleep well last night?"

Frank shook his head. "Just an hour or so."

"You only slept one hour?"

"But that doesn't bother me. When my brain cells are regenerating big-time like this I don't need much sleep. Sleep is mainly for undoing the knots of stress, did you know that? It's for resting the brain, not the body. When your body's tired, all you really have to do to recuperate is lie down. But if someone's stressed out and doesn't sleep for a long time they can turn savage, do things you'd never imagine people could do."

A girl I knew came into the bar. She was alone, and I waved her over.

Noriko was a tout for what they call an "*omiai* pub." "Omiai" means "matchmaking," and an omiai pub is a place where women are approached on the street and invited to come drink and sing karaoke for free. Male customers pay to come in and try to hook up with them.

"Well, if it isn't Kenji," Noriko said, walking unsteadily toward us. I introduced her to Frank.

"Noriko's an expert on the clubs around here. She'll tell us a good place to go."

In Japanese I told her Frank was a client of mine. Noriko had no English. She was about twenty, a dyed-in-the-wool j.d. who'd probably spent more time in reform schools than any other kind. I hadn't heard this from her, mind you—it was the sort of common knowledge you tend to pick up in a place like Kabuki-cho. Like all genuine j.d. girls, Noriko never talked about her own past, no matter how drunk she got. But just talking to her made you realize the term "juvenile delinquent" still meant something.

With the arrival of Noriko between us, Frank got one of those incomprehensible looks on his face. His eyes seemed to flicker with something that might have been anger or discomfort or hopelessness. Noriko glanced at him but immediately looked away. Women like her have an unfailing instinct for where not to look.

"Come to think of it, I still don't know your last name, Frank," I said as I paid for Noriko's drink. She'd ordered a Wild Turkey and soda.

Frank was looking more and more sullen by the moment. "Last name?" he muttered, shaking his head.

"Kenji," Noriko said, edging away, "are you sure I'm not in the way here?"

I gave her a pleading look and urged her just to stay for a while.

"Masorueda," said Frank.

At first I thought he'd said something in Japanese, like *Maa, sore da*. Eh? I said, and he pronounced it slowly—MA-SO-RU-E-DA. I've had close to two hundred foreign clients, but I've never heard a last name like that. Masorueda-san, I told Noriko.

"I thought his name was Frank," she said, pulling a pack of Marlboro reds from the pocket of her hooded duffel coat. She took a big slug of Wild Turkey and lit a cigarette.

"Frank is his first name, like Kenji or Noriko."

"I know that much. Like Whitney's the first name and Houston the family name, right?"

"How's business?"

"No good, too cold out there. You coming to our pub?"

"If this one wants to we will."

Frank was watching this discussion with his usual expressionless eyes.

"He's a gaijin, Kenji, don't ask his opinion, just drag him there. Don't you ever do that?"

"Not usually."

"You don't say."

"Why are you drinking so early? Finish work already?"

"Just started, stupid, but I got pissed off." Noriko held up her empty glass. "Can I have another one?"

Sure, I said. The bar was crowded, but over the noise you could hear a jazz guitar recording. Noriko knew a lot about jazz for someone of our generation. She was bobbing her head to the rhythm of the bass echoing off the walls and floor, with the smoke from her cigarette drifting up through her long, bleached, rust-colored hair. Noriko had striking, chiseled features, but she looked tired. Frank asked me if she was a hostess. I blanked on the English word "tout" and explained that she did the same sort of work as those black guys. She's pretty, he whispered to me. I passed this on to Noriko, who glanced at him and said: *"Domo."*

"That's Kenny Burrell on the guitar," Frank told her. "A piano player named Danamo Masorueda used to do a lot of sessions with Kenny Burrell. He's not a famous pianist, and not all that good, either, but he's from Bulgaria, and his grandfather was a sorcerer for a heretical sect called the Bogomils."

What's the gaijin-san saying, Noriko wanted to know, and I gave her a rough translation. So this piano player had the same family name? she asked, pulling out a second cigarette. Frank lit it for her. *"Domo,"* she said, then: "Ah, thank you!" She chuckled at her little adventure in English, and Frank blew out the match and countered with a *"Domo"* of his own.

Noriko then wanted to know what he meant by "sorcerer." "You mean like Siegfried and Roy?" she asked me.

"A magician?" I asked Frank. No, he said, and made a big deal of it by leaning back and waving his arms.

"You may know that sorcery was big in medieval Europe. Well, Bulgaria was the center of all that. I'm not talking about sleight of hand or juggling, I'm talking about black magic, Satanism, where you get power from the devil, not from God—you ally yourself with Satan. Tell her what I'm saying, Kenji. I'd think a girl like her would find this interesting."

Frank's eyes glistened as he talked about this stuff. They grew moist and red, and his eyelids fluttered slightly. I was reminded of the eyes of a dead cat I once saw when I was a little kid. Walking across a vacant lot, I didn't notice the cat and stepped on it. Its carcass was already starting to rot, and I felt its gas-filled stomach burst, and one of the eyeballs popped out and stuck to my shoe.

"It was all about sex, that's what they were really into, all types of abnormal sex—sodomy, coprophilia, necrophilia. The whole thing started in the fourteenth century, when the Knights Templar defending the roads to Jerusalem met up with a heathen Arab cult. Did you know that when new recruits wanted to join the Templars, the initiation rites required them to kiss their sponsor on the anus? I bet it would excite the young lady to hear stories like this. The Rolling Stones were into Satanism at one point. She looks like she'd like the Rolling Stones."

I struggled to translate this. What a crock of shit, Noriko said.

"I'm not interested in devils or whatever, but I know that's not Kenny Burrell on the guitar. I've never heard such crap. This guy's a *baka*, Kenji—listen to that guitar, anybody can tell it's Wes. This *baka* doesn't even know Wes Montgomery when he hears him." Noriko poked Frank on the arm and said: "*Baka da yo, Os-san.*"

After I'd given Frank a simplified translation of what she'd said, Noriko started shouting at me: "What about the *baka* part? Even I know the word 'fool,' and you didn't say it just now."

I told her there was more than one way to call someone *baka* in English, but she wasn't buying it.

Yakuza hoods are the classic example, but people like Noriko get this way sometimes. Drunk or sober, she always had a hair trigger, and you could never tell how she was going to react to anything you said. With no warning whatsoever, even when you've meant no offense, people like her will suddenly decide you're disrespecting them. If you just try to laugh it off they really snap, and once they've snapped there's no way to salvage the situation. I looked at Frank, and he was morphing into the Face again. There it is, I thought. There's the Face that first aroused my suspicions. Noriko glanced at him too, and I could see her thinking: What the hell is up with this gaijin? She stopped shouting.

"Kenji," Frank said in a low, thick voice. "Is this broad a prostitute?"

He's asking me if you sell it, I told Noriko. She peered at Frank as if trying to decipher him and said:

"Not anymore, but you'll find a lot of girls like that in our pub."

Frank turned the Face toward me as I translated.

"All right," he said. "Let's go to her pub."

On top of the table in front of each woman was a placard with a number on it. There were five of them, and they were drinking juice or whiskey-and-water and taking turns singing karaoke. Noriko poured Frank and me some beer, handed us each a postcard-size piece of paper, and explained the system. We were to write the number of the lady we liked on this paper, each sheet of which cost ¥2000. We could also write down what it was we hoped to do with the girl.

"Like, 'I'd like to take you out somewhere,' or 'Let's have a drink together here and get to know each other.' Just keep it clean," Noriko said. "These girls aren't pros."

"What's she saying?" Frank asked me. I murmured in his ear that the women were amateurs.

In terms of looks and fashion and attitude, they represented a variety of types. The woman behind placard #1 wore a white minidress and a lot of makeup and didn't look like an amateur to me. A non-professional, dressed like that, on her own in Kabuki-cho on December 30? It would have been inconceivable just three or four years ago. Lady #2 wore a leather jacket and velvet pants, and #3 a cream-colored suit. Ladies #4 and 5 were together and wore similar, brightly colored sweaters. Lady #1 had just finished singing, and now #3 was performing a Seiko Matsuda song from about ten years ago.

"Kenji, what kind of place is this?" Frank asked me. "She said we'd find hookers if we went to her pub."

I told him that in Japan right now there were more and more women who were somewhere in between pro and amateur, but I didn't really expect him to understand. Ladies #1 and #3 were smiling at me and Frank. Not even I could say with any certainty where on the pro/am scale they fell. The room had six or seven tables and muddy orange wallpaper with an incomprehensible design. A design that said: We wanted the place to look classy and tried to imitate the effect of tapestries in some European castle, but—sorry!—on our budget, this was the best we could do. A few pictures hung on the walls, reproductions of the kind of still-life paintings you might find in some small-town exhibition. The menu on the table had little illustrations of flowers in each corner and was handwritten and said things like: *Yaki-soba—wait till you taste our sauce!* and *Ramen—and we don't mean instant!* Next to the "kitchen area" (basically just a sink and a microwave) stood a middle-aged man in a suit who had to be the manager, and a young waiter with piercings in his nose and lip. There was one other male customer, in his forties or so, who looked like he might be some sort of civil servant.

"Which of them are hookers?" Frank asked me, ballpoint pen in hand. "I told you I want to have sex. Noriko said we'd find prostitutes here."

I was trying to decide which of these five would be most likely to leave the pub with Frank on a "date." All five of them were borderline—each looked as if she might be selling it or might be just a plain old office girl. Of course, no perfectly respectable woman would come to a place like this, but I'm beginning to wonder if there's still such a thing as a perfectly respectable woman in this country.

On the sheets of paper Noriko gave us was a box where you wrote the number of the lady you liked, then four larger boxes where you introduced yourself: *Name, Age, Occupation, Where you usually go to party*. Then: *What you would like to do on your date*. Underneath that were four possible replies the lady could choose from.

1. I'd be happy to accompany you anywhere!

2. Let's go out for a drink!

3. Let's have a drink here and see if we hit it off!

4. Sorry!

The sheet of paper was delivered to the lady you chose, and returned to you once she'd indicated her answer. Frank chose Lady #1, and I filled in the rest for him. *Name:* Frank Masorueda. *Age:* 35. *Occupation:* President of an importing firm. *Where you usually go to party:* Nightclubs in Manhattan. *What you would like to do on your date:* Spend a romantic and sexy evening together. I didn't want to choose anybody for myself, but according to the pub rules I had to, so I reluctantly wrote down #2. You had to pay the ¥2000 per sheet up front. Frank plucked a ¥10,000 bill from his imitation snakeskin wallet, and Noriko took it and delivered the papers to the respective girls. Ladies #1 and 2 studied Frank and me closely, then clenched their pens and pored over the paper as if it were a final exam.

Noriko was getting up to leave, saying she had to get back on the street, when Frank stopped her.

"No, please, wait just a minute."

"Now what?" she sighed, and plopped back down. As I translated, a sense of foreboding came over me.

"I'm grateful to you," Frank said.

"Don't mention it. It's my job, you know."

"As a token of my appreciation, I want to show you something really interesting. It has to do with mental energy. Okay? It won't take a minute. Watch my two index fingers."

Frank pressed his palms together, like you do before a Buddhist altar.

"See that? My left and right index fingers are the same length. Only natural, you say? But in thirty seconds, the right finger will be much longer. Watch carefully, now."

Frank shaped his hands into a gun—his two index fingers were the barrel—and pointed it midway between Noriko and me.

"Watch closely. My right index finger will slowly start to grow, longer and longer, like in the story of Jack and the beanstalk. It's actually growing now, but if you don't watch carefully you won't be able to see it. . . ."

I was on Frank's right, and Noriko was across from us. Frank had pushed up the sleeves of his sweater and jacket, and from where I sat I had a clear view of his left wrist and the back of his right hand. There wasn't much hair on the inside of his left wrist, and I could see that he'd applied makeup there, like a flesh-colored foundation. What was he covering up, I wondered. Frank was recounting the story of Jack and the beanstalk, and as I translated for Noriko I peered at his wrist. Beneath the makeup I could see these raised lines that at first I thought were a particular sort of tattoo—like Hell's Angels often give themselves, scraping the skin to make a swollen wound and then injecting ink. When I realized what they really were, every hair on my body stood on end. Suicide scars. I know a girl who has three scars like that on her left wrist. But Frank's scars were beyond belief. There were dozens of them, more than you could count, within a space of about two centimeters, and they went halfway around his wrist. How many times had that wrist been slashed, then allowed to heal, only to be slashed again? Just thinking about it made me feel like throwing up.

"Kenji, where are you looking?" At the sound of Frank's voice a shudder ran through me, and I looked up at him. "Never mind," he said, "just translate what I'm saying for your friend here."

Something was wrong with Noriko. Her eyes weren't focused, and a thick vein stood out on her forehead, throbbing gently.

"You will forget everything," Frank told her. "Do you understand? The moment you step out on the street, you will forget everything that happened here."

I didn't translate this faithfully. In fact I told Noriko the opposite of what Frank had said: that she'd remember everything.

"Kenji, you weren't watching my fingers," Frank said.

He gave Noriko's shoulder a squeeze and said "I love you," raising his voice a little, and Noriko's eyes came back into focus. She excused herself politely and walked out.

Frank grinned at me. "What were you looking at?"

Noriko had disappeared out the door long before I found my voice. Nothing, I told him, trying to sound calm, but it sounded more like a frightened yelp. I've always hated the occult and the supernatural, and as far as I'm concerned, putting people into a trance ranks right up there with the worst of that stuff. It disturbs me even to think about someone losing control of their own will. This was the first time I'd ever actually seen it happen.

"I was watching Noriko. I've never seen that kind of thing before."

My voice was quaking. I figured I'd just have to make it seem as if I was shaken up not because Frank was scaring the shit out of me but because I was so surprised to see someone be . . . I didn't know the word in English.

"Hypnotized," Frank said, pronouncing it with a strange British accent I'd never heard him use before.

"Frank, I don't get it," I said.

"Get what?"

"If you can do that sort of thing, why pay a woman for sex? You could have any woman you wanted."

It's not that easy, Frank explained. "At this time of year, when it's cold outside, forget about it. It doesn't work if they can't concentrate. Get one to concentrate, and, yes, she can become very . . . suggestible, let's say. But it's no fun having sex with a woman who's like a zombie anyway. No, I prefer prostitutes."

The waiter with the pierced nose and lip brought the replies from Ladies #1 and #2 back to our table. Each of them had put a check mark next to *Let's have a drink here and see if we hit it off!* If we'd like to join them, the waiter told me, we would each have to pay an extra table charge and buy the ladies' drinks. I asked Frank, who muttered: "Not much choice, I guess." We all moved to a table for four.

Lady #1 was named Maki and #2 Yuko. Maki said she'd dropped in here just on a whim, because she had the night off from her job at a "super-exclusive members' club" in Roppongi. Just to sit down it costs you sixty or seventy thousand yen, she said, clearly expecting us all to be impressed. I knew right away she was lying. Her face and figure and fashion and manner of speaking and carrying herself didn't fit the picture she was painting. I figured her for a hostess at a girlie bar who only dreamed of working in a super-exclusive club.

Yuko said she was a college student and was on her way home from a party with a group from her school. It was the first get-together for the members of this activity circle she'd joined, she said, but it was boring so she left early but felt kinda lonely and didn't have anywhere to go, and since she'd never been to an omiai pub before . . . Yuko looked old for a college student. I wondered why all the people you meet have to be such liars. They lie as if their lives depended on it. She couldn't speak a word of English. Wasn't there an English test among her entrance exams, I wondered but didn't ask. I was in no frame of mind for wasting my breath on stupid questions. "So—no English, huh?" Frank said, not making much of it, but Yuko reacted by looking down at her hands and very meekly saying that actually it was just a vocational school. This was probably the truth. The waiter came, and Yuko ordered an oolong tea and Maki a whiskey-and-water.

"Places like this never have decent whiskey," Maki said after sipping her drink. What that meant, of course, was that she herself normally drank super-exclusive whiskey in super-exclusive clubs. She was chattering away in Japanese as if it were the only language in the world.

"What do you usually drink?" Yuko asked me to ask Frank. Bourbon, he said. That was news to me.

At least I was able to get my mind off my worries to some extent by concentrating on translating back and forth. But I couldn't wipe out the images of Frank's scarred wrist and Noriko's hypnotized eyes. Frank had pushed his sleeves back down, and his wrists were hidden beneath his black sweater now. As for Noriko, some part of her had gone missing. The girl who walked out of here wasn't the same one who'd walked in.

"Oh, *baa-bon*?" Maki said. "What kind do Americans drink? Turkey and Jack and Blanton's, I suppose, right? Isn't that what they drink?"

It wasn't so much a question as an attempt to let us know how knowledgeable she was. Frank hadn't even registered that she'd said "bourbon," however.

It's a difficult word to pronounce, and the Japanese version doesn't come close. When I first started doing this work, Americans never understood my pronunciation of it. One guy even thought I was trying to say "Marlboro."

"The ones you just named are the ones they ship out. Down south, where bourbon comes from, they keep the really good stuff for themselves and don't export it. J. Dickens Kentucky Whiskey is probably the best example. An eighteen-year-old Dickens tastes like the finest cognac. You know, people often have a bad impression of the South, but there are a lot of good things about that part of the country."

Neither of the ladies had any idea what "the South" meant. Nor, incredibly enough, had they ever heard of the American Civil War. Frank was astonished that anyone could be familiar with several different brands of bourbon and not know about the Civil War, but Maki didn't display any embarrassment. "Who cares about that?" she said.

I glanced at my watch and realized I'd been with Frank for nearly fifty minutes and hadn't called Jun yet. I asked Yuko if it was all right to use my mobile phone in this place. "How should I know?" she said in a tone that meant *I'm not a hostess here, Mister.* Maki said: "It's all right, everyone does it, I talk on my mobile here all the time." Which of course told me she was a regular and probably at least a semipro. Frank and I were sitting side by side on a sofa, and the ladies were across the table from us. I don't know much about furniture, but I could tell the table and sofas and chairs were pieces of crap. There was a dismal aura of cheapness about them, which was only magnified by the tacky attempt to make everything look high-class. The sofas were too small, for starters, and the upholstery was unpleasant to the touch. You felt as if the dirt and grease and dead skin of all the previous horny, lonely customers were rubbing off on you. The table had that unmistakable sheen of particle board, but the surface was imprinted with a wood-grain pattern, as if that could fool anybody. I haven't seen much really good furniture in my life, but I know crappy stuff when I come in contact with it because it brings me down. Yet the sofas and tables matched the two ladies across from us so perfectly that I found myself coming up with a new proverb: *The ghosts of sad, cheap souls live on in sad, cheap furniture.* Maki carried a Louis Vuitton purse. It didn't suit her, but I couldn't blame her for trying. When you're using the genuine article—not just designer goods, but anything that's made really well —it never brings you down. It's not easy to know what's genuine and what isn't, though, so unless you're willing to go to all the trouble of refining your taste, you need to rely on brand names. I think that's why girls in this country are so obsessed with Vuitton and Chanel and Prada and the rest.

The sofa had these oddly shaped armrests that made it impossible to sit sideways or even cross your legs comfortably. I pressed my knees together, but my thigh was still plastered against Frank's. And I couldn't extract the mobile from my jacket pocket without my elbow and forearm coming in contact with his body. "You calling your girlfriend?" he asked. Yuko pushed a napkin and ballpoint pen across to Frank, saying: "Name, name, you, name." He absently wrote FRANK, then lifted the pen off the napkin and said: "Kenji, what was my last name again?" He smiled as he asked me this—a smile that would have given anyone the willies. Just then Jun answered the phone.

"Kenji! Are you all right?"

"Yeah." I was about to expand on that when Frank said, "Let me talk to her," and reached over and took the mobile from me. Instinctively I clutched at it, but he easily ripped it from my fingers. Like a hungry gorilla stripping a banana from a tree. What the fuck are you doing, I nearly shouted, but the survival instinct kicked in, and I shrank back down in my seat. If I were a dog I would have tucked my tail between my legs and rolled on my back. I was on Frank's right and had been holding the phone in my right hand when I saw his left arm stretch out in front of my eyes, all but covering my face. He grabbed hold of my wrist and pulled my hand away from my ear, then used his other hand to wrench the phone from my grasp. I thought he was going to tear off a few fingers along with it. It had been a very violent act, but it happened so quickly that the ladies must have thought we were just horsing around. "Oh, stop it!" they squealed with pseudo-girlish glee. Frank's strength was off the chart, and his hand felt the same way his arm and shoulder had the night before, when I was leading him out of the batting cage. Metallic. I was afraid he was going to crush the phone in his fist. Mind you, he'd done all this without any visible effort. It wasn't as if he was straining.

"Hi! My name's Frank!" he shouted into the phone, loudly enough to drown out the background music playing over the speakers—a song by the Ulfuls—but his tone was cheerful and friendly. Like the super-salesman type you often see working the phones in American movies. "You're Kenji's girlfriend, aren't you? What was your name again?"

I prayed for Jun to act as if she didn't understand English.

"What's that? I'm sorry, I can't hear very well—the music..."

"Hey, Frank," I said. I wanted to tell him Jun didn't speak much English, but he gave me an icy look and growled: "Shut up, I'm talking here!" The Face made a brief appearance, and it was scarier than ever. Maki wasn't looking, but Yuko happened to glance up and see it, and the smile froze on her lips. Even a dim-witted vocational school student with zero English could sense something abnormal in the Face. She looked like she was going to burst into tears. I, for my part, was learning this much about Frank: the angrier he got, the cooler he became. As his rage grew, his features seemed to sink and contract and his eyes would glint with a colder and colder light. Expressions like "boiling mad" didn't suit Frank at all.

"What's that? I'm asking what your name is! Your name!"

Frank was all but bellowing into the phone now. Apparently Jun was doing a good job of pretending not to understand.

"Kenji," Frank turned to me, "what's your girlfriend's name?"

I didn't want to tell him. "She's not used to talking to foreigners," I said. "She's probably... confused."

I wanted to say she was probably intimidated, but couldn't think of the word.

"What's to be confused about? I just want to say hello. After all, you and I aren't just a guide and his customer now, we're—"

The intro to a karaoke tune blasted over the sound system, several times louder than the background music had been. The civil servant guy started singing, and there was no possible way to carry on a telephone conversation. Frank spread his hands palms up in a disgusted shrug, then handed the mobile back to me.

"I'll call again, don't worry!" I shouted to Jun and shut the thing off.

"Why don't they turn down the music?" Frank said. "The noise is *brutal*."

To hear him use that word was somehow both funny and depressing. Like listening to a prostitute denounce promiscuity. But it was true, the karaoke had been turned up to a nearly intolerable level. The civil servant, a man in his mid-forties or so, was butchering the latest song by Mr. Children, and the girls were clapping along apathetically. He'd clearly chosen this song to appeal to them. Anyone could have told him that just singing a Mr. Children song wasn't going to make him popular with young women, but he was giving it all he had, belting out the lyrics so passionately that veins bulged in his throat. Frank gestured to me that it was too loud even to talk and sat there looking disgruntled. I was none too gruntled myself. I was concerned about Jun, and I was worried about Noriko out on the street and probably still in a trance, but more than anything I was consumed with my own distrust and fear of Frank. The last thing I needed right now was to have someone belt out, at earsplitting volume, a song I didn't even like. People in this country have no consideration for others, no glimmer of comprehension that they might be annoying those around them. There was something very ugly about this man contorting his face as he struggled with the high notes. It wasn't a good key for him, and in any case it wasn't a song he'd chosen out of an actual desire to sing it. He'd chosen it to ingratiate himself with the girls, and he didn't seem to notice that the girls were all but yawning and rolling their eyes. In other words, he was the only one who failed to realize that what he was doing was completely useless. And infuriating. I was getting genuinely pissed off and beginning to wonder if we really needed people like this in the world. For a moment I thought: He should be put to death, this guy. And at that very moment, Frank looked at me and nodded and smiled as if to say: *Exactly*. An electric shiver ran through me. Frank had been devising a new name for himself on Yuko's napkin. Having already written FRANK, he'd started to scrawl the O of DE NIRO when he gave me this conspiratorial glance. The timing was just like when you say to someone "I could kill that guy" and they shoot back, "Yeah, I know what you mean." What was going on with this guy? Had he really just read my mind?

Now Frank was shouting in my ear to ask me to interpret something for him. Yuko was apparently a big fan of Robert de Niro's, and had nearly wet herself when informed that Frank had the same last name.

"Kenji, listen, these girls don't speak any English. I want to tell them that Robert de Niro means 'Robert of the House of Niro.' " He spoke rapidly between choruses of the song. My pulse was galloping again. It was all I could do to say I'd tell them when the song was finished. The apprehensions that had been building inside me suddenly coalesced into one big ball of anxiety. I had a horrible feeling that something very bad was about to happen. Frank had changed—his appearance, his personality, even his voice. He'd given Noriko and me some phony name and tried to hypnotize us both. He'd sent her off in a trance, he'd hijacked my phone call to Jun, and now he was reacting to my thoughts as if by telepathy. What the hell was going on here?

The song finally ended. There was a pathetic smattering of applause, and the civil servant guy made the peace sign and went: "Yay!" I decided not to look at him. To pretend he wasn't even there.

When I explained the meaning of de Niro, Yuko gazed admiringly at the napkin and said that names were fascinating, weren't they? But Maki let out a nasty snorting laugh, like a sneer.

"They may share the name," she said, "but that's all they've got in common."

Of all the women you see in Kabuki-cho, Maki's type is the lowest of the low, if you ask me. Unattractive, riddled with complexes, and dumb as a post, but because of the worst sort of upbringing ignorant even of her own ignorance. Convinced she ought to be working in a classier place and living a better life, and equally convinced that it's other people's fault she can't pull it off. Envious of everybody else and therefore eager to blame them for everything. Treated so badly all her life that she thinks nothing of doing the same to others by deliberately saying things that hurt them.

"What did she say?" Frank asked me.

I told him.

"Oh?" he said. "And what's so different about me and Robert de Niro?"

"Everything," Maki said and snorted again.

I was at a loss. Should I make this idiot woman across from us shut up? Should I get Frank out of this pub? Or should I pretend I needed to use the restroom and run like hell? So many things had happened in so little time that I couldn't marshal my thoughts. The narrowness of the sofa had something to do with it. Because Frank's thigh was pressed right up against mine, part of me had already abandoned all hope of escape. When the body's constrained, so is the spirit. I knew this was no time for getting worked up about the karaoke singer or Maki, but when you're in an extreme situation you tend to avoid facing it by getting caught up in little details. Like a guy who's decided to commit suicide and boards a train only to become obsessed with whether he remembered to lock the door when he left home. All the same, I kept trying to devise a way of taking Maki down a notch or two. And I couldn't come up with anything. Women like her have a nearly impenetrable barrier of stupidity. I could put it to her straight—*You're a moron*—but that wasn't likely to produce much more than an angry *What's that supposed to mean?*

"Everything. Everything!" she said again, looking at Yuko for confirmation. "Right?"

"Um, I don't know," Yuko said, opting to keep it vague.

"But they're totally different. The face, the style, the body, everything." *Snort.*

"Have you ever met the real de Niro?" Frank asked her. "He's got a restaurant in New York, and I've seen him there two or three times. Bob's not that tall, and he's very unassuming, just a regular fellow. Jack Nicholson lives on the West Coast, which may be why he has that movie star air about him, but de Niro really seems like just a normal person. That's how you know he's a great actor. That mood, that intensity you see on screen, is something he has to work very hard to create."

I didn't see what good it would do, but I translated this too. Meanwhile the waiter with the piercings brought two orders of *yaki-soba* and potato chips to our table. I told him we hadn't ordered them. "*I* did," Maki said, snatching one of the plates of grilled noodles and veggies. "You have some too," she told Yuko.

"Kenji, did you translate what I just said?" Frank asked, watching the girls dig in. I told him of course I did. What were we doing here anyway, he wanted to know.

"Did we come here to watch two broads eat noodles? I want to have sex. Noriko said there were hookers in this place. Are these two hookers?"

I translated the question. "What a jerk," Maki said through a mouthful of noodles. "Right?" she said to Yuko. "That's what's wrong with places like this, you get all the losers, know what I mean?" Yuko gave me a troubled look before saying: "But I can see how he might misunderstand." "Don't be silly," said Maki, "we're not the ones who asked them to join us." She waved her hand dismissively as she spoke, and part of a sauce-covered noodle fell on her dress. "Shit!" she shrieked, wetting a handkerchief and dabbing frantically at the spot. "Bring me a hand towel!" she shouted at the waiter standing by the counter, loud enough to drown out the Ulfuls, whose album was back on the sound system. She scowled at the dark stain on her white dress and wiped at it with the moist cloth the waiter had fetched, but the stain wouldn't come out. Maki was short, with a round face and rough, swarthy skin. To think there were men who'd pay good money even for a woman like this. Men today are such a lonely breed that any woman who wants to sell it, as long as she isn't absolutely hideous to look at, will find a buyer. Which is partly why women like Maki get so full of themselves.

"Look what a pretty pattern it made," Frank said with a smile. I translated this.

"What's he talking about, he doesn't know anything!" Maki spat back, refolding the hand towel and dabbing at the stain some more. Yuko clucked sympathetically: "That's a Junko Shimada, right?" "That's right," said Maki, glaring at Frank and me and adding pointedly: "I'm glad somebody knows quality when they see it. You might not think it to look at me, but I've always worked in the highest quality places, even as a student working part-time, and not just nightclubs, either, my first part-time job was at a market in Seijo-Gakuen where they had nothing but the best gourmet foods that only rich people could afford, like sea bream sashimi, five slices in a pack, ¥2000. Tofu too, I couldn't believe it at first, they had tofu made by hand somewhere near Mount Fuji that they can only make five blocks of it a day, and it was ¥500 for one piece."

Making a point of ignoring Frank and me, Maki had turned to Yuko, the only one here who could possibly understand. Yuko nodded and sucked up her yaki-soba as she listened. Lady #4 was leaving. She'd been left on her own after the Mr. Children guy chose Lady #5. Of the five women present, #4 and #5 were dressed in the most conventional clothes—sweater and skirt, sweater and slacks—but as it turned out, they were the true professionals. The Mr. Children guy, familiar with places like this, had sniffed it out. The only one left alone now was Lady #3, who was holding the karaoke mike and leafing through a song catalogue. She was wearing a suit, but she was young. She was also the prettiest woman here. It was just past ten o'clock, so I figured her for a hostess on the late shift—midnight till four or five in the morning. This place was more like the waiting room in a train station or something than a pub: a random mix of men and women killing time till something happened. They say that not just in Kabuki-cho but in entertainment districts around the country there are fewer and fewer customers whose main goal is sex. I know of a street in Higashi-Okubo where older men form a queue for a chance to talk—just talk!—to high-school girls. The girls hang out in coffee shops on that street and get thousands of yen an hour for chatting with these guys. Lady #1, who was still going on about how she'd lived her entire life in contact with items of the very finest quality, had probably once done similar things. Maki sincerely believed that because she'd come up surrounded by ¥500 tofu and ¥2000 sashimi and whatnot, nothing but the best was good enough for her. Naturally the Junko Shimada dress didn't suit her in the least, but she didn't have a single friend who would point that out to her. Then again, even if such a person were available, she'd have made sure to avoid them.

I once heard a psychiatrist type say on TV that people need to feel they're of some value to go on living, and I think there's something to that. It wouldn't be easy to keep going if you thought you were of no use to anyone. I looked at the manager of this place, who was standing at the counter tapping away on a calculator. He might have been the prototype of men in the sex industry. You could tell by his face he'd long since stopped even asking himself if his life was of any value. Men like him, managers of soaplands and Chinese clubs and S&M clubs, not to mention gigolos and pimps—men who eke out a living exploiting women's bodies—all have one characteristic in common: they look as if something has eroded away inside them. I talked about this with Jun once but couldn't explain it very well. I tried to describe it in a lot of different ways, saying it was as though they've given up hope, or lost their pride, or lied to themselves too long, or have no emotions left whatsoever, but she didn't really get it. Only when I described their faces as blank—only then did she say she understood, kind of. About two or three weeks after that, I saw a news report on North Korea. It was about how people were starving there, and they had shots of some of the children. And in the faces of those skinny, dying kids was the same whatever-it-is that you see in the faces of men who live off the traffic in women's bodies.

The waiter, slouching against the counter next to the manager, wasn't in that category. Men who make a living off women don't pierce their noses and lips. He was probably in a band. The band not being successful enough to pay the bills, one of his buddies may have helped him land this job. There's an astronomical number of young dudes playing in bands, and in Kabuki-cho you can hardly spit without hitting one. Ours was miles away, his eyes staring at nothing anyone else could see. In a small voice, Lady #3 had begun singing an Amuro tune—something about how lonely everybody is deep down inside

—but the waiter didn't look at her, didn't even seem to be aware of the fact that someone was singing. Meanwhile, the Mr. Children guy had loudly and brazenly opened price negotiations with Lady #5, who I now realized was probably over thirty. The room was warm and she'd perspired a bit, dissolving some of her makeup, and you could see some serious wrinkles on her neck and around her eyes. Mr. Children was badgering her: I bet you work the telephone clubs, I've met loads of women like that, and I know one when I see one, honey. Maybe #5 was in desperate need of cash, because nothing he said seemed to piss her off. She sat with her hands on her knees, simpering and shaking her head from time to time or looking up at the door as if willing a more appealing man to enter. Something's wrong with me, I thought. I don't normally spend so much time studying other people, especially in places like this. Maki was still blathering away. Yuko had finished her yaki-soba. Frank asked me to translate what Maki was saying, and I did, mechanically.

"After I quit the job at the market I took some time off for a while and then I started working in nightclubs, but I told myself I would never work in a low-class place, because the only people you get in low-class places are low-class people, right?"

"Just a minute," Frank interrupted her.

"What?" Maki said, but her face said: Put a sock in it, Fatso.

"What are you doing here? What is it you came here to do? That's what I can't understand."

"I'm here to talk to people," Maki said. "I've got the night off at this exclusive club I work at in Roppongi and normally I don't come to Shinjuku that much but sometimes I come here just to talk to people, and people usually get a kick out of my stories because they're full of things hardly anyone knows about. When I say 'my stories' I mean like, for example, I'm the sort of person who even going to America or someplace I never want to fly economy, you know what I mean?"

She took a sip of whiskey and looked at Yuko for agreement. "Mmm," Yuko nodded, "some people are like that, aren't they." Yuko had been glancing at her watch a lot the past few minutes. Having left a boring party, she'd simply decided to pass the time at an omiai pub before heading home, and now she was planning her exit. Not being as hardened as Maki, she apparently considered it rude to bolt immediately after wolfing down the noodles we'd treated her to. She hadn't noticed that Frank and I were finding Maki very difficult to take, and as she timed her escape she was absently chiming in with a word or two whenever Maki paused to breathe. Yuko was thin, with a pale, unhealthy-looking face. Her flat, straight hair hung down over her collar, and from time to time she would flick it back with unmanicured fingernails. Though not particularly interested in what Maki was saying, she'd nod in agreement whenever called upon. She was more of a regular civilian than any other woman here, but she was here. Plainly no stranger to loneliness.

"If you ride in coach, the atmosphere of coach soaks right into you, that's what one of our regular customers told me, and I think it's really true, don't you? This customer is a man who works for a TV station, and believe me you'd never see him in a place like this. He says he's never traveled anything but first class in his life, and on domestic flights he always gets the SuperSeat, except Japan Air System doesn't have the SuperSeat, so when he wants to go somewhere only JAS flies to, he books a seat in the Green Car of a bullet train instead. I mean, there are people in this world who live like that. You may not realize it if you've never flown first class, but it isn't just about the seat being bigger. For example, did you know that if your flight is delayed or canceled, the way you get treated depends on the class you're in? They put everybody else up at a hotel right near Narita Airport, but if you're in first class they put you in the Hilton next to Disneyland. The Disneyland Hilton, can you believe that? It's always been my dream, to stay there—well, I guess that's true for everybody, right?"

Yuko acknowledged the question with another ambiguous *Mmm.* I was still mumbling into Frank's ear a translation of whatever bullshit Maki came out with, like a simultaneous interpreter. I'm not used to that sort of thing and don't really have enough English to do a very good job, so my translation grew rougher as Maki rattled on. The last bit, for example, came out something like, "All Japanese dream of staying at the Hilton," but I didn't think it mattered much.

"The Hilton's not such a high-class hotel," Frank said to Maki softly, as if to help correct a misconception, but depending on how you took it it might have sounded like a putdown. In fact, that's how I took it—I thought Frank was trying to dump on her. And that sort of nuance tends to leap language barriers. "You don't know much about anything, do you?" he told her. "Take the New York Hilton, for example. It's said that four hundred rooms is the maximum number you can have if you want to maintain the very best service, but the New York Hilton has over a thousand. That's why the truly rich never stay there. They prefer the European-style hotels, like the Plaza Athénée or Ritz-Carlton or Westbury. The only people who choose the Hilton are hicks from the country and Japanese."

Maki's face reddened. She didn't like being grouped with hicks. Which meant she was probably from the country herself. Yuko said: "Hmm, I guess there must be lots of things about America that only Americans would know."

Maki pushed her lips out in a pout. "So where is this person staying?" she asked me.

"I can't tell you that," I said.

Frank wanted to know what "the broad" was saying now. I translated the question, and he said: "The Hilton." Yuko laughed, but Maki just resumed her monologue, telling us how she'd stayed at all the finest hotels in Tokyo. How the front desk at the Park Hyatt must be hundreds of meters from the entrance, and how her room at the Westin in Ebisu Garden Place had the most comfortable sofa she'd ever sat on, and so on and so forth. She also made it clear that she only stayed in these places with important people like doctors and lawyers and TV station people, so in effect she was admitting to being a hooker after all, much to Frank's amusement. As she rattled on I noticed we'd been in this place for just over an hour now and asked the waiter for the hourly tally. He brought me a bill for nearly ¥40,000.

"What's this?" I said, and his mouth dropped open slightly, making his lip-ring jiggle. "That's not the price Noriko told us," I said, trying to speak in a calm, friendly manner so as not to cause any sort of scene. "Who's Noriko?" he said, then looked over at the counter where the manager was standing. He immediately glided over to us and inquired in a hushed, deep voice if there was any problem. I asked him to bring a breakdown of the bill, but he already had it with him. The original table charge was ¥2000 apiece, the charge to change tables and sit with the ladies ¥4000 apiece (doubled because we'd stayed longer than one hour), the yaki-soba was ¥1200 per, the potato chips ¥1200, the oolong tea ¥1500, the whiskey ¥1200, the beer ¥1500, and in addition to sales tax they'd added a service charge.

"I wish you'd told me when an hour was up," I said.

Frank looked at the breakdown and shouted: "That's insane!" He couldn't read the Japanese, but he could read the figures. "I've only had two whiskeys, and Kenji, you only drank one beer!"

They were on an hourly system here, the manager explained in his funereal tones, but as we could see, they were a bit short-handed, so they couldn't really be responsible for keeping track of how long each customer had stayed. "I'm sure you understand," he said. I understood all right. Shafted. No matter what I said, he would point out that they were merely charging the standard amount according to the pub's clearly outlined system. And if I continued to complain, a specialist would show up and suggest we discuss the issue in the back office. End of "discussion." I told Frank there was nothing we could do. He nodded: "So that's the type of place this is." I said yes, I was afraid so, but none of this was strictly illegal so it was useless to argue.

"I'll explain it all later. But this is partly my fault, so feel free to deduct half the bill from my fee."

I was really willing to let him do that. It was my responsibility to watch the clock.

"Never mind," Frank said. "Let's just pay up for our time so far."

So far? I thought. Frank pulled four ¥10,000 notes from his snakeskin wallet and handed them to the manager. They were the oldest, filthiest bills I've ever seen. The manager held them between one thumb and forefinger, a look of disgust on his face. The bills were heavily stained and caked with greasy dirt and seemed on the verge of disintegrating. I remembered hearing rumors that some of the homeless in and around Shinjuku Central Park had packets of money stowed away among their bags and rags.

We all stared at the bills. None of us, I'm sure, had ever seen anything quite like them before.

"There," Frank said, "now we're paid up for so far."

"What do you mean 'so far'?" I asked him.

He wanted to stay longer, he said. The manager, who'd obviously done his share of time in Kabuki-cho, must have sensed something disturbing about Frank's face and attitude, not to mention the unbelievably dirty money. Generally, he said, their customers liked to wrap things up at about this point. Translation: Please leave. "Frank, let's go, the system here is for us to finish up now," I told him, clapping him lightly on the shoulder. The muscles there were as hard as cast iron, and a chill ran from my fingertips all the way down my spine.

"All right, then, shall we move on?" he said. "Oh, wait—those bills I just gave him, I dropped them in the gutter earlier, maybe I should pay with a credit card?"

He pulled out his wallet again as the manager, recognizing the words "credit card," gave him a quizzical look.

"Kenji, ask if I can use a card."

A credit card is fine, the manager said warily.

"I have a really unusual American Express card. Look at this. See? You girls look, too. Seriously, lean in here. Now look closely at the card. There's something unusual about the face of this warrior fellow, right? If you move it back and forth like this in the light... Look there. It looks like he's smiling, doesn't it? Now watch carefully...."

The two staff members and the pair of women leaned closer and closer to the card, as if pulled toward it. A familiar, creepy vibe told me that Frank was up to something again. The air seemed so dry it pricked my skin, yet so dense it was hard to breathe. I, for one, wasn't going to look at Frank's card. I kept my eyes on the manager and waiter, and sure enough in a matter of seconds I saw a change come over them. Something in their eyes. I once read that when you're hypnotized you temporarily enter the world of the dead, and whether it's true or not, I do know that *something* spooky happens. I saw the manager's pupils dilate as he stared at the Amex card. Then, a moment later, the muscles of his jaw and cheeks tensed up so tight you could hear his teeth grinding, and veins stood out on his neck. It was the expression of someone absolutely petrified with fear, but it lasted only a few seconds. Then the veins deflated and the light went out of his face.

"Kenji," Frank said in a very soft voice. "Step outside and call your girlfriend."

"Huh?" I said, and he repeated it slowly, enunciating the words.

"Step. Outside. And call. Your girlfriend."

The Face was gone. Frank looked strangely radiant, like someone who'd finally finished a long and difficult job and was now about to celebrate with a cold beer. The manager, the waiter, and Maki and Yuko were all in a trance of some sort. The waiter's lip-piercing jiggled as if in a small breeze, but he looked like a mime frozen in position. Everyone's eyes were unfocused, and I couldn't tell if their muscles were relaxed or tense. Maybe both at the same time. Meanwhile, Lady #3 was still singing, and Mr. Children was still negotiating with Lady #5. None of them seemed to notice the extraordinary atmosphere surrounding our table.

"Frank," I said, nudging him, "that's not cool." I assumed he intended to leave everyone hypnotized and walk off without paying. "We can't run out on the bill. I'll never be able to show my face in Kabuki-cho again."

"I wouldn't do anything like that, Kenji. Just get out of here and let me handle this, will you?"

Or do you want me to kill you? his eyes seemed to say. My spine felt as if it were packed in ice, but before I knew it I was on my feet, which made me wonder for a moment if I'd been hypnotized too. I turned sideways to squeeze past the manager and waiter. It was like threading my way between a pair of mannequins. My elbow brushed against the waiter's right hand, but he wasn't there to feel it. As I walked away from the table I glanced back at Maki and Yuko. They were both leaning forward in their chairs, rocking back and forth as if on seesaws.

I walked out the door toward the elevator hall and flipped open my mobile. I knew Jun would be in my apartment, but I couldn't bring myself to call her and just paced up and down awhile. Finally I walked back and peered inside the pub through a tinted glass panel in the door. I could vaguely make out shapes moving around inside. And then I saw an unmistakable form lumbering toward me. I dashed for the elevator, but it was too late.

"All right, Kenji, come on back in," Frank said.

I didn't want to go. But with Frank's eyes drilling into me, I couldn't have moved anyway. I had turned to stone, from the tip of each hair on my head all the way down to my toenails. Frank grabbed me by the shoulder and dragged me inside. At the door I lost my balance and nearly fell, but he caught me and easily supported my entire weight with his right arm. He carried me inside as if I were a piece of luggage and dropped me carelessly on the floor. I heard him walk back to the door and pull down the steel security shutter outside it. When I opened my eyes I saw two pairs of legs, a man's and a woman's. I knew the woman was Maki by her red high heels and white lace stockings. A wet, shiny, scarlet line slithered down the shin of one stocking. Like a living creature, some sort of parasite maybe, it was crawling along the delicate threads at a slow but steady pace. At a table facing her, Lady #5 along with Mr. Children and Lady #3 sat goggling slack-jawed at Maki. The moment I looked up and saw what they were staring at, everything in my stomach began the journey back up my esophagus. It looked as though Maki had another mouth below her jaw. Oozing from this second, smiling mouth was a thick, dark liquid, like coal tar. Her throat had been slit literally from ear to ear and more than halfway through, so that it looked as if her head might fall right off. And yet, incredibly, Maki was still on her feet and still alive, her eyeballs swiveling wildly and her lips quivering as she wheezed foam-flecked blood from the wound in her throat. She seemed to be trying to say something. The man beside her was the manager. He and Maki were leaning against each other, as if they'd been positioned to hold each other up. His neck was twisted in an unnatural way, his head turned as though to look over his shoulder, but drooping limply, chin resting on his shoulder blade. Just beyond Maki's high heels, Yuko and the waiter lay in a heap on the floor. A thin blade, like a sashimi knife, was buried deep in Yuko's lower back, and the waiter's neck was twisted like the manager's.

Lady #3, Mister Children, and Lady #5 sat as still as cardboard cutouts on their sofa, but I didn't know if they were hypnotized or unconscious or just paralyzed with fear. I struggled to hold down the vomit rising inside me. An acid wave washed up through my chest and throat, and my temples were numb and tingling. I couldn't think, let alone speak. This can't really be happening, I told myself. It was like being in a nightmare you're sure you can't awaken from. Frank moved into my line of vision, walking toward Lady #3. He had the long, thin knife in his hand now, having extracted it from Yuko's body. Apparently Lady #3 was neither unconscious nor hypnotized, because she reacted to Frank's approach—but in the oddest way. Her right hand, still grasping the mike on the sofa cushion beside her, began to jerk frantically back and forth, as if she were pawing at the material. Like a kitten excited at play. The mike was still on, and the sound of it rubbing over the cloth reverberated through the room. She was trying to run away, I thought, but her will was disconnected from her body. Her shoulders shook from the tension in her face and neck, and though the muscles of her legs were straining so hard you could see them bulging, she couldn't so much as wiggle her toes. The nerves connecting her brain to her muscles had short-circuited, and the movements of her body were random and uncontrolled. I was in a similar state—my vision and hearing were messed up. The backing track to the

Amuro song Lady #3 had been singing was still on, but I wasn't sure I was really hearing it with my own ears. When Frank stopped in front of her, #3 soiled herself explosively beneath the skirt of her cream-colored suit. As her fluids sprayed over the floor, all the strength drained from her body. Her feet fell out of her strapless shoes, her shoulders drooped, and her face relaxed into something like a smile just before Frank grabbed her by the hair and plunged the knife into her chest. And like a gnat flying out of a clump of grass, something went missing from that peculiar smiley face.

That's when Lady #5 at last began to scream. It wasn't like a reaction to #3's murder specifically, but rather as if someone had finally hit a switch to turn on the volume. Frank pulled the knife from #3's chest and then tried to take the mike from her, but her fist was so tightly clenched that even he had trouble prying it loose. Her fingers had turned white and puffy, as if they'd been pickled. Frank grabbed her by the hair again and rammed his index finger into her eye. I heard the sound it made from where I lay, and simultaneously I saw her hand release the mike. Something the like of which I'd never seen came out of her eye socket. A thick, gooey, semitransparent liquid speckled with red dots. Frank took the mike and held it up to Lady #5's screaming mouth. This amplified the scream many times over, of course, but also made it sound, strangely, like a song. He pointed at #5's throat and looked at me. You could see her vocal cords vibrating as she screamed. Signaling me with his eyes as if to say "Ready? Watch this," Frank sliced deeply into the vibrating flesh, and the scream dissolved in a loud *shoosh*, like escaping steam.

Frank seemed to be moving in slow motion one moment and fast-forward the next. At times it was as if he was barely moving, and at others, like when he pulled the knife from Yuko's back, things happened with bewildering speed. It's amazing how easily your senses and reflexes can become deranged when you're in shock. The woman sitting beside Mr. Children had just had her throat slit, and he'd watched it all as if it were a Cup Noodle commercial. He wore an expression that was beyond hopelessness. I once read how in extreme situations your body releases these hormones—adrenaline and whatnot—that speed up your pulse and make you tense and excited at the same time, ready to fight or flee. But a body and brain accustomed to normal, mild reactions just get confused and disjointed when this flood of hormones is released. I think that's what was happening to me and everyone else in the room. When I remembered the can of mace in my breast pocket, I agonized for a moment, wondering if I shouldn't take some sort of action to stop Frank, but the very idea was unbearable. Instead, I had the weirdest thought: of just running into the restroom and throwing the little can away. Whatever it may have symbolized, that mace in my pocket was utterly powerless in the face of the reality Frank was causing to unfold. The instant I'd realized I was going to be murdered, the possibility of action had gone right down the drain, and watching the knife plunge into #3's chest and seeing #5's throat yawn open like the hood of a car, my body had completely seized up. It was as if every nerve in my system had frozen solid. I couldn't even imagine screaming for help, let alone trying to run, and you can't do something you can't visualize yourself doing. Normally we don't notice it, but we always have to picture ourselves doing something before we can match the image with an action. And that was what Frank had made impossible—he'd destroyed our ability to visualize a course of action. Not many people in this country have ever seen a human being's throat sliced open. There just isn't the wherewithal to think how cruel it is, or to feel sorry for the person, or to be horrified, or even to tell yourself, you know, *That's gotta hurt*. The slashing of Lady #5's throat produced very little blood, oddly enough, but you could see this dark red slimy stuff inside the wound. Probably the severed vocal cords. You might spend your whole life without ever seeing such things in the raw, but when you do see them you instinctively recognize them as something you have inside yourself. And take it from me, once that happens you lose the power to visualize your next action.

When blood finally began oozing out of the crevice in #5's throat, it looked black, not red—exactly like the soy sauce you use with sashimi, I thought. I was still unable to move, paralyzed, and my neck and shoulders and the back of my head felt numb and cold. I probably wouldn't have been capable even of turning away if Frank had poked his knife in my face. There were no windows in the pub, but on one wall was an enormous video screen, and on it I could somehow visualize the street outside—a world where people still lived and talked and walked around, now hopelessly out of reach. I felt I was already knee-deep in the world of the dead. Outside, people were buying and selling sex. Women were standing on corners in miniskirts, legs covered with goosebumps from the cold, trying to rent out their bodies, and men were laughing and singing drunkenly as they shopped for a woman to relieve their loneliness. Under the twinkling neon lights touts and barkers were calling out to the drunks walking by: *We promise you a good time!* I saw this vision as if through an unfocused lens, and I tried to face the fact that all of that was gone forever now.

Frank grabbed Mr. Children by the hair and turned his head so that he was facing Lady #5. Her head was tilted back, not only widening her wound but stretching the skin of her throat so that it was taut and smooth, like the tanned hide of some animal. Held by his hair and forced to absorb this sight, Mr. Children, astonishingly, screwed his face into a smile and laughed: Heh, heh, heh. It was like when you see victims of earthquakes or typhoons on TV, and they're smiling. "You think this is funny?" Frank asked him. The man couldn't have understood, but he nodded sheepishly several times and laughed again: Heh, heh. Then, with Frank still holding him by the hair, he decided to have a cigarette. He picked his pack of Seven Stars off the table and extracted one. Frank watched closely as the man put the cigarette in his mouth and searched his trouser pockets for a lighter, as though he were just having a little smoke to calm his nerves. Frank reached for the lighter on the sofa next to Lady #5, fired it up, and raised his eyebrows as if to say *This?* Mr. Children nodded, smiling again, and Frank turned up the flame and held it to his eyes and forehead and hair. A smell of scorched tissue wafted over to me. The man struggled to get away from the flame, but Frank only gripped his hair more tightly. When he took the flame away for a moment, the man's lips trembled and he smiled again, nodding repeatedly as if in gratitude. Frank then held the flame to his nose and lips, and this time he struggled a little more violently. He flapped his arms about and tried to avert his face, and like an infant throwing a tantrum he pounded Frank's stomach and chests with his small fists. "Keep it up, go wild," Frank muttered as he roasted the man's face. Then, to my utter disbelief, he yawned. It was one of the biggest yawns I've ever seen, splitting his face open like an egg. At last Mr. Children began screaming. His scream faded in and out, like a poorly tuned radio. Frank moved slightly to one side to allow me a clear view, perhaps guessing that I'd never seen a burning human face before. The orange flame was licking the insides of the man's nostrils. The Amuro song had ended at some point, and now a tune by Takako Okamura was playing. Mr. Children looked like he was trying to dance, waving his arms and legs to the music. Frank glanced at me as if to say, *Hey Kenji, check it out.* The flesh around the man's nose was melting like wax and dripping in a thick, brownish goop with occasional little flaming gobs of fat, while the sweat poured from his temples and forehead. His face was turning purple, the tip of his nose was beginning to char, and I could clearly make out a crackling sound, like a scratchy old LP. The entire area around his nostrils became so black you couldn't distinguish the holes from the charred flesh, and then his screams died out and his arms dropped to his sides. I could hear the Takako Okamura song and the crackling flesh and a third sound which I only gradually recognized as Mr. Children weeping. His jaw shuddered and shook with his gurgling sobs. Frank looked at him curiously, before giving another yawn—long and leisurely and so cavernous that it looked like he was going to swallow the man's head.

Mr. Children still hadn't lost consciousness when Frank left off burning his face and reached over to hike up the skirt of Lady #5, whose throat was still leaking blood. The moment Frank lifted her skirt she slumped against the backrest of the sofa. Her head flopped back over it until all I could see of her face was her nostrils, and then, carried by its own weight and with a sound like a rusty lock giving way, it flopped even farther. I never would have thought the head could bend all the way back like that. Now the wound looked like the mouth of a vase filled with dark-red fluid. I could see veins and bone and a gooey white stuff, but strangely enough the blood still wasn't spurting but only slowly seeping out. Mr. Children was holding his molten nose with his right hand as he sobbed. Tears and sweat dripped from his face, and some fluid matter oozed through his fingers. Frank spread Lady #5's legs apart, then ripped her panties and stockings open and waved me over, saying: "C'mere, Kenji." I didn't go. I was still sprawled on the floor and literally couldn't have moved to save my life. Frank let go of Mr. Children's hair, strode over to me and, grabbing the collar of my jacket, dragged me across the floor to #5's feet. Her body was twitching in various places. Maybe she was still alive. The flesh quivered where her inner thighs met her groin, and her pubic hair bristled as her vagina opened and closed, for all the world as if it were breathing. "Kenji, tell this man to have sex with her," Frank whispered in my ear. I shook my head. I'm not sure I could have spoken anyway.

"Tell him!" Frank shouted.

Along with the fear I felt an overwhelming revulsion. Frank had the long, thin knife in his right hand and held it up before my eyes. The numbness in my temples intensified, and the nausea that had caught in my throat surged up to my back teeth. And when my eyes fell again on #5's vagina wriggling like a shellfish, I spewed a cappuccino-colored stream onto the floor. As I puked, I felt my anger rising. I don't think the anger was directed at Frank precisely. It was more of an abstract, absolute sort of anger. NO, I tried to say, but only managed to spill dribbles of vomit from my mouth. I spat out some of the sour, sticky stuff adhering to my tongue and gums and inner cheeks. To do this, though, I had to arch my back and splutter for all I was worth. Frank was looking down at me with obvious amusement. "Better yet, Kenji, why don't *you* have sex with her?" he said. "Go ahead, fuck her." He pointed at #5's vagina with his knife as he said this. I spat once more. It required the concentration of my entire being to get the nerves and muscles to connect and cooperate. But when I saw my spit hit the floor, I felt the welcome return of what seemed like long-lost circuitry. I don't know exactly what it was I'd recovered: my will, maybe, or maybe just the ability to release tension. But whatever it was, I knew it was something you couldn't do without if you wanted to be in control of your own body. Without it you were at the mercy of your environment, like some sort of plant. I could feel my voice gathering.

"NO!"

I tasted flecks of vomit on my tongue as I pronounced the word. I'd managed to clearly visualize the letter N and the letter O and to picture myself sounding them out, and, lo and behold, out came my voice. I said it again: "NO!" I felt I had to make my will known to this gaijin. Just expressing something to someone wasn't necessarily the same as communicating. I'd never really realized that before. A while ago, Lady #3 had scraped the microphone over the sofa like an infant having a tantrum, and Lady #5 had begun "singing" just moments before getting her throat cut. You might say these were signals the women were using to try and express something, but naturally they failed to get their meaning across to Frank. You can't communicate anything with random signals like that. Before Frank had turned up, this pub was like a symbol of Japan, self-contained, unwilling to interact with the world outside, just communing with itself in every breath—*mmm, ahhh*. People who've spent their lives living in that kind of bubble tend to panic in emergencies, to lose the ability to communicate, and to end up getting killed.

"No?"

Frank made a big production of acting as if he couldn't believe his ears. He looked up at the ceiling, spread his arms wide, and shook his head. I don't know why this particular thought occurred to me at a time like this, but I thought, yeah, he's an American all right. The Americans, like the Spanish, massacred millions of Indians, but I don't think it was out of malevolence so much as plain old ignorance. And sometimes ignorance is even harder to deal with than deliberate evil.

"What did you say, Kenji? 'No'? That's what it sounded like to me. Is that what you just said? '*No*'?"

Frank was slowly waggling the knife in front of my face. I was at his feet on my hands and knees. When you're in a groveling posture, groveling words are the only sort that come to mind. I wanted to change positions but couldn't very well move with that knife in my face. "NO!" I said yet again, still on all fours. The smile on Frank's face sagged into a sorrowful frown.

"Kenji, you don't understand."

He swung the knife back toward Lady #5's vagina. It looked to me as if he was winding up before sticking it into me. I thought: I'm done for.

"You don't know how good it feels to have sex with a woman who's dying, or who's just died. It's the ultimate experience, Kenji! The brain's dead so they can't resist, but the pussy's still alive."

There was something very mechanical and singsongy about the way he was speaking, like a bad actor reciting lines he'd learned years ago, to see if he can still remember them. A white thread was entangled in Lady #5's pubic hair, and I suddenly realized it was the string to a tampon. I'd never actually seen that before. Well, she wouldn't be needing tampons anymore. That frayed white string seemed to symbolize a life cut short. Lady #5 was fair-skinned, but the flesh around her vagina was turning pinkish gray.

"Kenji, you disappoint me."

Frank turned and placed the long blade of his knife behind Mr. Children's right ear, then sliced downward, lopping it off. The man had been sitting with his face in his hands, and his right thumb fell away with the ear. His cries didn't get any louder as a result. To be frightened, to weep, to feel pain—those things require energy, and Mr. Children didn't have any left. Frank sighed as though bored and cut off his other ear as well. It fell to the floor soundlessly, like a slice of fishcake or something, and lay there among the loose strands of hair and cigarette ashes.

"All right, Kenji," Frank said, "you don't have to have sex with her. But how about picking up that ear and sticking it in her pussy? You can do that much, can't you?"

He said this quietly, sounding almost despondent now. "Ever crammed an ear into a pussy before?" he asked me. I didn't answer. His face was expressionless as he put the knife down on the sofa, plucked the dust-covered ear off the floor, folded it, and tried to insert it in Lady #5's vagina. He didn't seem to realize she was wearing a tampon. He had about half of the ear buried inside her but was meeting resistance. I called to him. He pushed harder.

"Frank. Hey, Frank." I rose to a crouch. "It was that time of the month for her. She's wearing a tampon."

Frank peered at me, then nodded and removed the ear. He curled the string around one finger and tugged. When the little cylinder, swollen and pink, slid out to dangle at the end of the string, a thick ooze of blood followed and soaked darkly into the sofa between her legs. Frank stared at that little pool of blood for a long time, as though mesmerized by it. While he was doing this, Mr. Children went *Oooh* and made as if to stand up. He wasn't trying to escape—it was more like he'd suddenly reawakened to the pain where his ears and nose had been. Frank snapped out of his reverie and turned to him. Still dangling the tampon from his right hand and holding the ear in his left, he took the man in his arms as if embracing a lover and broke his neck. I heard a dry crack, like a dead branch breaking, and with his head twisted at the now-familiar angle, Mr. Children plopped back down on the sofa. It was murder with all the drama of picking up a fallen hat and replacing it on a rack. Frank looked at me, dropped the tampon, and retrieved the knife. He wore a petulant expression as he stepped toward me, like a small child who's tired of playing. The pointed end of the knife was closing in on my throat when my mobile phone rang. I scrambled to push the blinking green button. Frank hesitated for a moment, then brought the knife closer to my throat.

"Jun? Yeah, it's Kenji, I'm in Kabuki-cho, with Frank!"

I rattled this off in English, in a loud voice, and Frank retracted the knife a centimeter or so. I kept talking, raising my voice even more.

"Try me again in an hour, and if I don't answer, call the police!"

Before shutting off the phone I heard Jun shout: "Kenji, wait a minute!" I didn't have a minute, though—the blade was nearly touching my throat.

This was the first time I'd taken a good, close look at the knife that had just killed four women. The blade was only about two centimeters wide, but maybe twenty centimeters long. I remember thinking that it was longer than my penis when erect—but I can't tell you why I had such an idiotic thought at a moment like this. The base of the blade was engraved with the mark of some sort of fish. Maybe it was the type of knife fishermen use to clean their catch. The handle was cream-colored, like ivory, with wavy grooves on the bottom to fit your fingers. Incredibly, Frank's fingers and hands hadn't so much as a drop of blood on them, despite the used tampon and the severed ear and all the rest. Now that I thought about it, it seemed he'd taken special care not to muss himself, handling the ear, for example, as if it were something breakable as he tried to insert it in the woman's vagina. I saw no blood on his clothes or face, either. Obviously Frank had mastered a technique for cutting throats without spraying blood. Not even the slash straight across #5's larynx had caused anything like the crimson geyser you see in movies. The tip of the knife began to waver slightly. Frank was muttering something under his breath, and I closed my eyes. For the first time I became aware of the smell of blood all around me, so strong that I could hardly breathe. It was like the smell in a metal shop—that metallic dust in the air. I remembered the warehouse I went to with Dad, and its rows of giant machines. I saw Mom's face, too. The thought of how sad she'd be when she heard I was dead made tears well up in my eyes, but I instinctively felt I mustn't cry. There are bastards in this world evil enough to commit murder just to watch others weep. For Frank it clearly wasn't only that, but I wasn't about to risk inciting him by whimpering and wailing. I crouched there with my eyes closed, not daring to move a muscle. I felt a light tap on my shoulder.

"All right, Kenji. Let's go."

Frank said this softly in my ear. Like somebody who'd had a pleasant enough time and was now ready to move on to the next diversion. For a moment I thought that when I opened my eyes I'd find that nothing had really happened, that I'd imagined or dreamed it all. Maki would be blathering about super-exclusive clubs and liquours, Mr. Children would be hitting on Lady #5, Lady #3 would be singing her Amuro song, the waiter's lip ring would be jiggling, and the manager would be adding up the tab and looking grumpy. I heard Frank say: "Kenji, wake up, let's get out of here." I turned my head to one side to avoid seeing his face and opened my eyes. It wasn't a dream. Right in front of me were Lady #5's gaping wound and Mr. Children's broken, twisted neck.

3

Frank raised the steel shutter to let us out, then pulled it down again behind us and said: "Did that scare you?" As if we'd just ridden the new roller coaster at Magic Mountain or something. My answer—and even I couldn't believe I was saying it—was: "A little." I think my body, and my nervous system, were trying to get back to normal. They wanted me to let it go, forget about it—what was done was done. Frank didn't have the long, thin knife in his hand anymore. Had I seen him slip it into an ankle-sheath? I seemed to remember that, but the memory was as vague as something from a dream.

"Well, shall we?" said Frank, hooking his arm around my shoulder and stepping out onto the street. I might have shaken him off and run away shouting MURDERER!—but I didn't. I couldn't. It was as if my nerves were still curled up in a ball. My knees and hips throbbed with a dull pain, like you get when you lie in bed all day, my pulse felt weak, and my vision was still messed up. Everything was blurry, and the familiar blinking neon lights of the sex clubs seemed to stab at my retinas. I found myself keeping an eye out for Noriko. Would she snap out of her trance at some point? Even if she remembered all about meeting me and Frank, and discovered what had happened in the pub, I was fairly sure she'd vanish rather than cooperate with the police. Noriko was probably on probation and not allowed to work in the sex industry.

"Kenji." Frank pointed at the police box near the corner. "Why don't you run over there and tell the cops what happened?"

To have him more or less confirm in words what he'd just done put a tremendous amount of stress on me somehow, and I was suddenly trembling all over.

"Kenji, you know, I've told you nothing but lies so far. I hope you won't hold it against me, because the truth is I can't help it. My brain doesn't work right and I can't connect the memories in my head very well. And it's not just memories, either, it's me myself. There are several me's inside this body, not just one, and I can't get them to connect, or merge. But I'm pretty sure the me I am right now is the real me, and you may not believe this but the me I am now can't understand the me who was inside that pub a while ago. You're probably thinking, where does he get the gall to make excuses like this, but I honestly feel it wasn't me doing those things, it was somebody else who looks exactly like me. It's not the first time he's done that, either. I've been trying to make sure it didn't happen again, though the only strategy I could come up with was to not lose my temper. When they cut out part of my brain, like I told you yesterday, that's what started it all, according to the doctor the police sent me to. The police, yes. I've been caught before, and sometimes that's part of the punishment, being put in a psych ward. But believe me, I've been punished in plenty of ways, by both God and society."

He kept his eyes on the police box as he spoke. We were both leaning against a cinderblock wall between two buildings, and the police box was about twenty meters away, next to a pharmacy with a garish neon sign flashing DRUGS DRUGS DRUGS. At a glance you might not have recognized it as a police box. It was a new structure, and so much bigger than most police boxes that it could have passed for the entrance to a small hotel or recital hall. But a number of policemen were milling around inside it, and now and then a cop passed through wearing a bulletproof vest. The rumor was that even the big windows were bulletproof. Only in Kabuki-cho.

"I'm going to buy myself a hooker now." Frank looked over at the few scattered ladies standing in the shadows of buildings across the street. "My last sex," he added, contorting his face into a lonesome-looking smile.

He took the snakeskin wallet from his jacket pocket and handed me most of the ¥10,000 bills inside. Ten or twelve of them, judging from the thickness, but I stuffed them in my pocket without counting.

"That leaves me ¥40,000," he said, shifting his gaze between me and one of the streetwalkers. "Is that enough?"

"Should be," I said. "The going price is ¥30,000, plus the cost of the room."

Frank headed across the street, and I followed, not knowing what else to do. I'll translate for you, I told him, and Frank said: You don't get it, do you.

"You don't get it, Kenji. I'm not your client anymore. You're free, go ahead and go to the police, tell them I'm a criminal. I'm tired, Kenji. So tired. I came to Japan looking for peace. Peace of a sort I thought I could find only here. But now I've gone and done something really out of line. What's to become of me? I want to leave it all up to you, Kenji. I'm entrusting my fate to you, my only Japanese friend. That is, of course, if you still think of me as a friend."

The word "peace" had a compelling reality coming from Frank's lips. I could feel the weariness and pain behind it. And call me a fool, but I believed him. I don't think my brain was functioning properly yet.

"You understand now?" Frank said, and I mumbled, "Yeah."

He left me there and moved toward the hooker. Most of the women on this street were Asians who for one reason or another weren't able to work at the Korean and Chinese clubs that specialized in organized prostitution. Some of them were shockingly old, but all of them, it was safe to say, had been cut loose by the yakuza who'd arranged for their visas and employment. A few were from South or Central America and had probably ended up here after being ostracized by their colleagues down the road in Okubo, where many of the hookers were from places like Colombia and Peru. The woman Frank was now negotiating with looked to be one of these, but apparently they were managing to communicate. I heard snippets of his broken Spanish—*tres* and *cuatro* and *bien* and so on. The woman smiled at him shyly from time to time. A woman like her, I thought...

A woman like her turns to prostitution because she has no other means of making money. Which isn't the case with high-school girls involved in compensated dating, for example, or the ladies in the omiai pub. Most Japanese girls sell it, not because they need money, but as a way of escaping loneliness. That seems particularly unnatural and perverse to me, compared to the situation of all the women I know who made it here from mainland China only by having relatives pool their resources to come up with the price of an airplane ticket. What's even more perverse is that nobody seems to acknowledge how out of whack this state of affairs is. Whenever the "experts" talk about compensated dating their main concern is to put the blame somewhere else. They pretend it has nothing to do with themselves. The Latin American woman Frank was negotiating with wasn't even wearing a coat in this freezing weather. No stockings, either, just a scarf over her head, like the Little Match Girl, and she was carrying only a vinyl tote bag, something you'd take to the beach. Women like her were selling the one marketable thing they had, simply to secure the bare minimum their families needed to survive. It's not a good thing, but it's not unnatural or perverse.

I was getting back some feeling in my body and turned up my collar against the cold. I could feel the icy, late December air on my skin, and this sensation marked a border between me and the outside world that I was glad to have back. Not that I'd fully recovered, of course, but as I watched Frank and the woman talking, one of the many filmy layers covering Kabuki-cho fell away, and I seemed to regain the ability to focus my eyes. Frank had told me to go to the police. My memory still wasn't working very well, but I was sure that's what he'd said. Why would he say that, though? I was leaning against the cinderblock wall again, between a love hotel and a stray girlie bar. Few people were on the streets tonight, what with the cold and the fact that tomorrow was New Year's Eve, and even the touts were relatively inactive. A noodle shop famous for its incredibly spicy ramen, which people actually queued up for in summertime, was closed, and a mangy, skinny dog lay huddled against the darkened glass door. In front of a sushi bar, with its metal shutter pulled halfway down, an apprentice chef was hosing vomit off the sidewalk. And the sputtering neon sign of a love hotel slashed pink and yellow wounds across the shiny body of a Mercedes, the only car in the parking lot.

No sooner had I regained my ability to feel the cold than I noticed how incredibly thirsty I was. I crossed the street and bought a can of Java Tea at a vending machine. From there I had a good view of the pharmacy and the police box. Frank and the woman were some distance down the street in the opposite direction, near the entrance to a love hotel. How come I wasn't running over to the cops and reporting what had happened? Somehow that course of action didn't seem to have any reality for me, and as I wondered why, I glanced back toward the hotel and saw that Frank and the Latin American woman were gone.

It made me uneasy to lose sight of Frank. I even thought about going to look for him, then thought again: He was a fucking murderer. The police box was still no more than thirty meters away. I could be on the other side of that bulletproof glass in twenty seconds—much less if I sprinted. I heard my own voice say: *What are you waiting for? He's a murderer, a brutal, merciless mass murderer, an evil man....* Evil? Well, wasn't he? What was I waiting for? I took two steps toward the police box. I'd once read an article about a little girl in England who'd grown so attached to her kidnapper that after she'd been rescued she claimed to like him more than her mummy and daddy, and a bank teller in Sweden who fell in love with the man who robbed the bank and took her hostage. The article said that in extreme situations like this, when a criminal literally controls whether you live or die, you can develop a feeling of intimacy with him that's very much like love. Frank hadn't hurt me. He'd grabbed me by the hair and collar and thrown me to the floor, but he didn't break my neck or cut off my ears. Still, that was no reason not to go to the police. Murder isn't something you can just turn a blind eye to. I took three more steps, and my feet stopped again. I hadn't decided to stop, my feet just took it upon themselves to do so. They didn't seem to want to go to the cops. I drained the rest of my Java Tea. *Do you have a problem with Frank being arrested?* I asked myself. The answer came back loud and clear. *Hell, no,* a voice said. *Wouldn't bother me at all.*

Whose voice is that? I muttered, and lifted the can of tea to my lips again, though it was empty. Not a drop was left, but I did this two or three more times before noticing. Maybe I should telephone someone. But who? *Who?* said the voice. I took out my mobile, and a picture of Jun's face formed in my mind. Not Jun, not now. Yokoyama-san? What would I say to him? *Yokoyama-san, the guy turned out to be a murderer after all, and now I'm thinking about going to the police. Do you think I should? I should, right?* I looked up and down the street. Frank was nowhere to be seen. The cityscape around me didn't seem real. It couldn't have been a more familiar place—one of the streets off Kuyakusho Avenue in good old Kabuki-cho—but I felt as if I was adrift in a strange town in some foreign country. It was like losing my way in a dream. I reminded myself I was still in shock, still not completely in control of myself. A uniformed cop came out of the police box, climbed on a bicycle, and pedaled this way.

I was sure he was staring at me as he approached. He was the only thing alive and moving in the universe. My legs had seized up again. It felt as if the circulation was cut off down there and the blood wasn't getting to them. As if they weren't even my legs. I was freezing from the waist down, but the cold wasn't the problem. I lifted the can of tea to my lips again but tasted only metal. I remembered the intense smell of blood in the omiai pub, and suddenly felt dizzy. The policeman reached the intersection, and without thinking about it I raised the mobile to my ear. Pretending I was on the phone. Instead of turning right, toward me, the cop hung a left and pedaled off down Love Hotel Lane. I watched him go, still mashing my ear with the mobile. The bicycle seemed to take forever to make the left turn but then sailed past another girlie bar at the corner and vanished. And once he'd disappeared from sight, I found I wasn't quite certain I'd actually seen the cop ride by in the first place. In a while my ear began to hurt and I realized I was crushing it with the phone. I had the phone in my right hand, the Java Tea can in my left. The can was moist and clammy. My palms were sweating, and the mobile too was wet when I finally pried it away from my ear. I hadn't realized I was sweating, and wondered if the tea had seeped straight out through my pores. That's when it dawned on me that I wasn't going to the police box. *I don't have to report to the stinking cops*—it was incredible what a relief this thought was.

Explaining the situation to the cops would have been a pain in the ass of epic proportions. A pain in the ass, I muttered to myself, and heard myself chuckle. How many hours—no, days—would the police grill me? It wouldn't escape their notice that I was a tourist guide without a license. That would probably spell trouble for Yokoyama-san, too. And when the whole story came out it would destroy my mother. Not only would the police forbid me to work, they'd now be keeping an eye me. I know how they operate. I'd be treated from the start as a probable accomplice. It would destroy Mom, I thought again . . . and then I thought of Lady #3. Naturally she and Mr. Children and the others had families too. I remembered their corpses, and their final moments. These images flickered through my mind like drug flashbacks, but unaccompanied by any real sense of revulsion or outrage. I remembered the sound of the guy's neck bones cracking, but all I could think was: So that's what it's like when you break somebody in two. Maybe my nerves still hadn't thawed out. I tried to feel sorry for the people who'd been killed but found, to my horror, that I couldn't. I couldn't feel any sympathy for them at all.

I'd spent two evenings with Frank but had only just met the people who died in that pub. I wondered if the reason I couldn't sympathize with the victims was that I'd come to empathize with Frank, but that didn't seem true. I had no affection for Frank. I don't think it would have bothered me if he were arrested, or even killed. But those people in the omiai pub had been like androids or something. Lady #2, Yuko, had said she was there because she felt "kinda lonely." She would actually have preferred to be doing something else but had no idea what that might be so decided to check out a matchmaking pub and at least talk to somebody. Lady #3 was the same. She didn't know what she wanted to do, so she ended up singing an Amuro song all by herself in that lonely place. Mr. Children was intent only on hooking up with Lady #5, whose only reaction to insults like "I can tell you're the type of broad who works those telephone clubs" was a simpering grin. The manager had been the classic Kabuki-cho lifer. Utterly resigned, the type of guy who'd numbed out his feelings of jealousy and futility to such a degree that even if his woman or the woman of a friend were to do whatever with another man, he'd be able to let it go. The waiter, on the other hand, was one of those young-dude-in-a-band types. He wouldn't have known anything much about music or ever tried to learn, having joined a band simply because he wanted friends. They were like automatons programmed to portray certain stereotypes, those people. The truth is it had bugged the hell out of me just to be around them, and I'd begun to wonder if they weren't all filled with sawdust and scraps of vinyl, like stuffed animals, rather than flesh and blood. Even when I saw their throats slit and the gore oozing out, it hadn't seemed real to me. I remembered thinking, as I watched the blood drip down from Lady #5's throat, that it looked like soy sauce. Imitation human beings, that's what they were. Lady #1, Maki, had never once given any thought to what was really right for her in her life, simply believing that if she surrounded herself with super-exclusive things, she'd become a super-exclusive person.

What did I have in common with the victims? Just that we were all human trash. I couldn't kid myself—I wasn't so different from them. That's why I understood them, and that's why they bugged me so much. At the entrance to the girlie bar diagonally across from the police box stood a young barker in a silver lamé suit and red bow tie. He was rubbing his hands together for warmth and calling out to everyone who passed. Above him was an arch of sequentially lit neon that made his face glow orange one moment and purple the next. When no one was on the street, he'd step back and yawn, and a minute ago I'd seen him tickle a passing cat behind the ears. My job was guiding foreigners to bars and strip joints and date clubs and helping them hook up with women. Nothing to be proud of and nothing that distinguished me in any way from the guy in the silver suit. But after nearly two years of working with foreigners, I'd discovered one thing: what makes somebody nice or unpleasant to be around is the way they communicate. When people are fucked up, their communication is fucked up. The communication in that omiai pub was all lies. It was a bar in Kabuki-cho, of course, which more or less precluded anyone telling the full truth or discussing serious issues. But that's not what I mean. Women in Chinese or Korean clubs, for example, will think nothing of lying to you if it means a better tip, but most of what they make they send back home, investing their capital in prolonging the lives of family members. It's the same for Latin American prostitutes in Japan—they sell their bodies to buy things for the folks back home. These women are serious and focused, because they know exactly what they want. They don't dither or feel lost, and they don't feel "kinda lonely." You wouldn't show your child a place like that omiai pub. Not because it was depraved or whatever, but simply because the people in there weren't living life in earnest. It wasn't as if the place had something any of them couldn't live without. They were just killing time there because they were "kinda lonely"—even the manager and waiter, really. All of them had been like that, not really living even when they were still alive.

I had no interest whatsoever in going to the cops and putting myself through a big pain-in-the-ass ordeal for people like them, but at some point I found myself walking toward the police box again. Part of me had surrendered to the inevitable. I couldn't very well go searching for Frank in the love hotel. I couldn't go back to my apartment and tell Jun: *Guess what, I saw some people murdered tonight.* Going to the police was the only possible course of action. But I hadn't taken more than a few steps when a horrible feeling came over me. My body was sending me a signal. A danger signal.

It seemed to be coming from my feet, or maybe one of my internal organs. Something wasn't right about this. I began to see that I was falling for something I never would have if shock hadn't scrambled my senses. That I was fooling myself, in other words. I had reached the cinderblock wall again, and as I leaned against it I decided to run through all that had happened, to try and get it straight in my mind. I didn't see much point in trying to understand what had triggered Frank to suddenly start slaughtering people. There was no way I'd ever understand that, no matter how long I puzzled over it. But why hadn't he murdered me? Call me in an hour, I'd told Jun—in English so Frank would understand—and if I don't answer, go to the police. I had no idea how much time had passed since then, pathetic as that may sound. I looked at my watch. It was just past midnight. Tiny specks of blood clung to the crystal, some of them not quite dry. Had Frank spared me because of Jun? Was he afraid she'd call the police?

As I was asking myself these questions the fear came creeping back. I felt I was on the verge of uncovering something my conscious mind didn't want uncovered. My mind was refusing to remember the really scary stuff. The fear had crept up through the soles of my feet and shivered through all my sinews, and now it was surging against my temples. Sheer, unbridled terror makes it hard to think clearly, and my brain was refusing to do its job. *Think,* I commanded myself. But just remembering Frank's face and voice turned my stomach, and suddenly I was vomiting. The Java Tea numbed my throat as it came back up and gushed from my mouth. I recalled that when Frank was in the midst of his killing and I was paralyzed with fright, unable to move or respond, I'd managed to get a small part of myself back by spitting forcefully. I hacked up a mixture of tea and saliva, and spat. It must be because of Jun that Frank didn't kill me, no other reason made sense. I didn't believe he felt any differently toward me than the others. Or even if he did, it wasn't to the extent that he'd hesitate to kill me. The point of that long, thin knife had been closing in on my throat when Jun called. And yet, what did Frank say to me just a while ago? "Go to the police, Kenji, I'm putting my fate in your hands." *He's lying again.* No sooner did this thought crystallize than the hair on the back of my neck stood up, and I turned around to see Frank. And only Frank.

He was standing right behind me, between me and the police box, blocking my vision entirely and so close that it was like he was preparing to absorb me. By some miracle I managed to remain both conscious and on my feet. Frank seemed much bigger than before. He was looming over me, and looked as if his weight alone could crush me like a bug, should he decide against swallowing me whole. I felt like a miniature version of myself.

"What the hell are you doing, Kenji?"

His voice wasn't very loud, but it nearly lifted me out of my shoes. Hadn't he gone into the love hotel with that Latin American woman? A car came down the street. Its headlights illuminated Frank's face as he spoke again, and this time I saw something in his mouth.

"Why didn't you go to the police?" he said.

He was rolling something around on his tongue.

"Is that gum you're chewing?"

Don't ask me why I asked him that. I was neither responding to his question nor ignoring it. I mean, it wasn't what you could call conversation. I don't think I was mentally capable of conversing just then. It was more like pulling your hand away from a hot fying pan—an automatic response. No chain of reasoning. I'd simply reacted out loud to the first thing that caught my attention—that stuff in his mouth.

"Oh, this?"

Looking pleased that I'd reminded him, Frank spat the thing out into his hand and showed it to me. It was like a ring made of ivory or something, in the shape of a snake swallowing the sun.

"That woman gave it to me. She's from Peru, but she speaks a little English. She said they find this substance in the sea, near the Incan ruins. What did she call it again? Lime sponge? Made of the bones of sponges with a high lime content, which they harvest and process and mold into these lozenges. Excellent source of calcium. Apparently the Mayans, the Toltecs, and the Aztecs all practiced cannibalism because their diet lacked calcium, but the Incans didn't, not so much because they had llamas and guinea pigs but because they had this lime sponge. Did you know calcium relaxes you, makes you more emotionally stable? She really understood me, that woman. Wasn't it nice of her to give me this? When I suck on it I feel totally at peace."

Frank was beaming. He wiped the lozenge off on his sweater and held it up before my eyes.

"Frank, are you sure she gave it to you? You didn't kill her and take it?"

I was shocked that I'd said this. It was as if a separate person were asking these questions. Both my own voice and Frank's seemed to reverberate, as though we were inside a cave. My heart was palpitating so bad I couldn't even feel the separate beats, and I thought my jaw was going to shake itself right off its hinges.

"I didn't kill her."

Frank looked off down the street. The woman with the vinyl bag was standing there, in pretty much the same spot as before. He gave her a little wave, and she waved back.

"Where'd you go?" I asked him. My voice was still saying things all by itself. "I lost sight of you both."

Frank said they'd stood in the entrance to the hotel talking awhile, then circled around behind the building and watched me from just over there.

"Oh, is that where you went!" I said. And to my own astonishment I smiled at him. "I thought you'd gone inside the hotel with her."

It wasn't like deciding to say something, choosing the words, putting them together into sentences in my mind, and then speaking. It was like I'd loaned my body to someone else, and they were doing the talking for me. I wondered again if I wasn't in some sort of trance.

"Frank, did you just hypnotize me?"

"No," he said, looking puzzled.

I was honestly afraid I was losing my mind. Blathering away without showing any other evidence of brain activity. I had no will or intention to speak, but the words kept popping out of my mouth. The trembling in my jaw was getting more severe, and trying to stop it just made it worse. My teeth began to chatter like castanets.

"You all right, Kenji?" Frank said and peered at my face. "Your eyes look funny, and you're shivering. Are you sick? Kenji, it's me, Frank! Do you know who I am?"

I laughed and said in a strangely high-pitched voice: "Frank, that sounds funny coming from you!" The words echoed in my skull, and I couldn't stop laughing for a while. Now I know I'm going mad, I thought. My brain was in utter chaos, with different parts of it seeming to operate independently. One part was searching furiously for words. It didn't seem to matter what the words were as long as they kept turning up, and any random memory or thought that happened along was automatically verbalized. It was as if my speech function was the only thing that still worked, and it had seized the opportunity to take control. If a dog passed by right now I'd probably say: *Oh, look, a dog*. Then I'd probably remember my boyhood pooch and tell Frank: *I had a dog when I was small.*

"Are you going to kill me?" I asked him. Exactly like a little kid, blurting out the first thing that occurred to me. But to my amazement I got some feeling back in my jaw when I said this.

"I was going to," he told me, "but I decided against it."

Tears welled up in my eyes. I bowed my head, not wanting Frank to see. As my teardrops fell to the dry pavement, I thought: It was only fear. It was fear that had befuddled my mind. At the sudden reappearance of Frank, I'd just lost it. All this turmoil was caused by fear. A fear so powerful I didn't even recognize it for what it was. It had filled my entire body and brain, and instead of screaming I'd begun nattering away, randomly and involuntarily. Just because Frank said he'd decided against killing me didn't mean he wouldn't, of course, but even if it was a lie it relieved the fear for a moment. I wiped my eyes with the sleeve of my overcoat. I wanted to say: *Really? You really won't kill me or anything?* But I didn't. I reminded myself he could always change his mind. The police box was behind Frank. If I ran for it now, I knew he could grab me and snuff me out before I took two steps. Mr. Children had had his neck broken in a heartbeat. Besides, my kneecaps were still bouncing around. I couldn't have run if I tried.

Frank threw an arm around my shoulders and off we went, with him all but carrying me. He looked back once at the Latin American prostitute, and she waved again.

"What a swell lady she was," Frank sighed, as if remembering an old friend.

The next thing I knew we were strolling past the glass-walled police box, bathed in the pharmacy's gaudy lights. At the entrance were traditional New Year's decorations of pine sprigs and bamboo and woven straw and cloth, which looked to me like symbols of everything imbecilic in this world. Inside, three policemen drank steaming cups of tea and talked and laughed. Meanwhile, I thought, a mass murderer fresh from the kill is walking right past you. The cops didn't know anything. Not that they should or could have. The security shutter was closed at the omiai pub, and no one who happened by would think twice about that. Even if Noriko's hypnosis wore off and she went back to the place, she'd probably just assume they'd decided to close early for one reason or another. It's not as if anyone would suspect that the place was littered with corpses. It might be days before anybody discovered or reported anything. Frank turned his poker face toward the police box as we passed and asked me again why I didn't go to the cops. I told him I was just going to when he appeared. Aha, said Frank, popping the lozenge back in his mouth. Everything was very strange. It was as if the universe had cracked open and time had got scrambled. As if the Great Omiai Pub Massacre had happened a decade ago and everyone but me had long since forgotten about it.

"Is it because you think of me as a friend?" Frank asked solemnly after looking back a couple of times at the police box receding behind us. "Is that why you didn't report me?"

"No," I said truthfully. "I don't really know why I didn't go."

"It's a citizen's duty to report any crime he witnesses. Did you think I'd kill you if you did?"

"No. I thought you'd gone into the hotel. I didn't realize you were watching me."

"Oh," Frank said, then muttered: "It's a good thing we didn't miss each other."

Miss each other? I thought. How can I miss you when you won't go away?

"I wanted to test you," he said. "Whether you really considered me a friend or not. That's why I left you alone by the police box and watched from nearby. I thought if I saw you going toward it all I had to do was kill you. You see, in my book nobody reports their own friends to the cops, and anybody who does deserves to die. But what do you think, Kenji? You think it's okay to rat on your friends?"

I don't really know, I was going to say, when my mobile rang. A truck was approaching, and it was noisy on the street, so I huddled against a wall, cradling the phone in both hands, and turned it on. It was Jun.

"Kenji?"

"Yeah, it's me."

"Are you all right?"

"Yeah, I'm fine."

"I meant to call earlier, but I was on my way home. Sorry."

"That's all right, don't worry about it."

"Are you with Frank?"

"That's right, still in Kabuki-cho. It's good you decided to go back home."

"I was a little worried. I mean, when I called earlier. You said something in English about the police and then hung up before I could say anything. And before that, when you called me, Frank got on the line and . . . What was going on, was he drunk?"

"Drunk, yeah."

"You said something about going to the police if you didn't answer, but I didn't know what I was supposed to tell them. 'There's this gaijin named Frank, and my boyfriend's with him, and he seems like a dangerous guy'—I mean, it's hard to imagine they'd take me seriously."

"You're right, they wouldn't have."

"Kenji?"

"What?"

"Are you really okay?"

"I'm fine."

She didn't say anything for a few seconds. Then:

"Kenji, your voice is shaking."

Frank was watching me with his usual blank, cowlike expression.

"I'll call again later," Jun said. "Or you call me. I have my mobile, and I'll be waiting up to hear from you."

"Okay," I said and turned off the phone, wondering if my voice had really been shaking just now. I thought I had it under control. Apparently I wasn't even in touch with what was going on with myself, I needed someone else to tell me. I wished I had someone who was absolutely rock-steady to compare myself with—someone I liked and trusted, if possible. To have them tell me that I was acting a little weird or that I seemed perfectly fine or whatever. It was strange talking even briefly to Jun because it gave me a glimpse of who I used to be in the old days, before the Great Omiai Pub Massacre. When I turned off the phone and looked at Frank, though, I felt as if I were being dragged right back into the hole I'd just crawled out of. I'd experienced the sunlit world for a minute, and now I was back in my prison cell.

"Is she at your apartment?" Frank asked as we started walking again. No, she went home, I told him, and he went: *Hmm.* No intonation—he might have been signaling relief or disappointment. But with Frank you had to expect your worst premonitions to come true. I was now positive that he knew where my apartment was, and that he was the one who'd plastered that scrap of skin on my door. Jun's house was in Takaido, though, and I doubted he could have found out the address. He can't get to her, I thought.

"That Peruvian woman has been in Japan for three years," Frank said as we ambled along. "She's had sex with almost five hundred men in that time, about four hundred and fifty Japanese, and some Iranians and Chinese. She's Catholic, you know, but she's decided that Jesus loses his power in this country, and I can kind of understand what she means. I can't explain it very well but I think I understand. And last year at this time she had an amazing experience that proved to be her salvation. Kenji—is it true that they'll ring the salvation bells all over Japan tomorrow night?"

At first I didn't know what he was talking about. The bells, he said—the gongs.

"She had a lot of bad experiences. I don't mean she was beaten or assaulted or anything, but apparently for her the hardest part about living here was all the group pressure, and the fact that people don't understand about personal space. The Japanese surround you in groups and talk about you behind your back in groups and don't think anything of it. They don't think about the pressure they're putting on you, and it's no use complaining to them because they don't even know what you're talking about. If they were openly hostile you could counterattack, but it's not like that, and she doesn't know how to deal with it. Like this one thing that happened when she'd been in Japan about six months and was finally picking up a little of the language. She was walking across a vacant lot surrounded by little factories and warehouses, and some kids were playing soccer there. Soccer's big in Peru, of course, and when she was a little girl in the slums near Lima they used to play with tin cans and rolled-up newspapers and things because they couldn't afford a ball. So watching these kids made her happy, it brought back good memories, and when the ball came rolling over toward her she tried to kick it back to them. But she was wearing sandals and the ball veered off to one side and landed in a ditch full of some kind of factory waste, and it got covered with this greasy gunk and smelled terrible, so she fished it out and apologized to the kids and was about to leave when they said: 'Hold on a minute.' They surrounded her, and told her she had to buy them a new ball, because this one was filthy and smelly and they couldn't use it anymore, but she couldn't even get her mind around that, because where she grew up everybody's so poor the idea of compensation didn't even exist, and she ended up breaking down in tears right there in front of the kids. She knows that women who come here to peddle sex aren't exactly welcome, but she realizes that would probably be true in most countries, and she's tough enough to put up with being sneered at or treated badly just for doing what she has to do, but she couldn't understand these kids demanding she buy them a new ball. There are sixteen people in her family and she came to Japan to work so she can rent them a small apartment in Peru, and she can't return until she's saved a certain amount of money, but at this rate she thought she'd never get ahead at all, and she didn't know who to turn to. This was her first time abroad, and she decided that since it's a foreign country they must have a different god and that maybe the god the Catholics pray to loses his power here because the customs are different, not to mention the land itself."

As Frank talked, we had slowly made our way past the west exit of Seibu Shinjuku Station through the canyon of skyscrapers and on toward Yoyogi. Now we turned down a narrow street with small wooden apartment buildings on either side. There wouldn't be any hotels in this area. The street was dark, and the buildings were crammed so close together that you couldn't see the skyline beyond them. The skyscrapers of West Shinjuku were still nearby but completely blocked from view, and above us the sky was flat, like a strip of dark blue paper. I walked at Frank's side, but he was leading the way. Walking helped calm my mind a little, and I found the story of the Peruvian prostitute oddly gripping. It was a subject close to my own heart, and it was also the first time I'd heard Frank speak with so much composure, or say anything that felt real and true.

Was it really because of Jun that he didn't kill me? Now that I thought about it, it couldn't have that much to do with her. All Jun knew about him was that he called himself Frank and claimed to be an American. Frank surely wasn't his real name, and anyway there must be hundreds of foreigners named Frank in Tokyo alone. Just as Jun had said, the police couldn't really do anything even if she did go to them. They had no photos of him, and no one knew his passport number or even if he was really American. The only people who could testify that he was ever in the omiai pub were dead except for me and Noriko, and I was one hundred percent sure Noriko wouldn't go to the cops. In other words, there was nothing to stop Frank from killing me tonight and taking a plane back home from Narita tomorrow. He could have killed me any time he wanted to, but he didn't.

"She thinks the Japanese need to do some deep thinking about their own gods, and she's right."

Who would have guessed you'd find a neighborhood like this, full of old wooden apartment buildings, pretty much smack dab in the middle of Tokyo and only about a fifteen-minute walk from Kabuki-cho? Not me. Amid the tenements were a few ancient, one-story wooden houses, like the kind you see in samurai dramas, so small I almost wondered if they weren't scale models. They had little sliding doors you couldn't have used without stooping, and tiny pebble-covered gardens. Some of the gardens had pint-sized, zinc-lined ponds, their surfaces rippling not with goldfish or carp but schools of slimy little pink things. Over the roofs of these low-slung houses you could make out the highrise buildings of the new city center in Shinjuku. Frank marched along at a steady pace, as if he knew exactly where he was going, and turned down a street that might or might not have been wide enough for a single compact car to pass. He kept going on about the Peruvian streetwalker.

"She wanted to find out about the gods of this country, but she couldn't find any books on the subject in Spanish, and she doesn't read English, so she asked a lot of her customers, but apparently none of the Japanese knew anything, which made her wonder if people here never came up against the kind of suffering where you can't do anything but turn to your god for help. The person who told her about the salvation bells was a Lebanese journalist who'd been here for over thirty years. He told her there was no figure like Christ or Mohammed in Japan, or any god like the kind Westerners imagine, but that certain big rocks and trees and things were decorated with straw ropes and worshiped as gods, and that people also worshiped the spirits of their ancestors. And he said she was absolutely right, that the Japanese had never experienced having their land taken over by another ethnic group or being slaughtered or driven out as refugees—because even in World War II the battlefields were mostly in China and Southeast Asia and the islands of the Pacific, and then Okinawa of course, but on the mainland there were only air raids and the big bombs—so the people at home never came face to face with an enemy who killed and raped their relatives and forced them all to speak a new language. A history of being invaded and assimilated is the one thing most countries in Europe and the New World have in common, so it's like a basis for international understanding. But people in this country don't know how to relate to outsiders because they haven't had any real contact with them. That's why they're so insular. According to the Lebanese man, Japan's just about the only country in the world that's been untouched, except for the U.S. But he said of course there's a bright side to that too and started telling her about the bells, saying that precisely because the Japanese have never experienced a real invasion, there's a certain gentleness here you can't find in other countries, and that they've come up with these incredible methods of healing. Like the bells. Ringing them at temples on New Year's Eve is a custom that goes back more than a thousand years, right? How many times was it they ring the salvation bells? It was a funny number but I forget what it was, a hundred and something, I think. Kenji, do you know how many times they ring them?"

Frank was talking about *Joya-no-kane*, the New Year's bells. A hundred and eight, I said.

"That's it, yeah, a hundred and eight."

We'd reached the end of a cul-de-sac, and I followed Frank into a narrow gap between two buildings. No light from the houses or streetlamps made it into this space, and it was so narrow we had to shuffle along sideways. The path ended at a ruined building that looked as if it had been in the process of being torn down by the land sharks when the real-estate bubble burst. Mortar had fallen from its outer walls, which were draped with canvas dropcloths and sheets of vinyl. Frank parted the sheets, and we crouched down almost to our knees to pass through into the building. The rain-splattered vinyl smelled of dried mud and animal shit.

"Last year she went to listen to them, and she said it was a transcendent experience, like being in another world, and that the hundred and eight bells washed away all her bad instincts."

Once inside the building, Frank turned on the light—a bare fluorescent unit on the floor—and his face, lit from below, became a puppet show of creepy shadows. The building must have been a clinic: in one corner was a pile of discarded medical equipment and broken chairs. A bare mattress lay on the hardwood floor, and Frank sat down on it and gestured for me to sit beside him.

"Kenji, those bells, they wipe out all your bad instincts, right? Will you take me to a good place to hear them?"

"Sure," I said, thinking: There it is—that's why he decided to let me live.

"Really? Thanks. So how do these bells purify you? She had a rough idea, but I want to hear it from a Japanese person."

"Frank, can I stay here tonight?"

I was pretty sure he wouldn't let me go home.

"There are beds on the second floor you can sleep on. I use this mattress here. I guess you must be tired—so much happened today. But I'd like to hear a little more about the bells, if it's all right with you."

"Sure," I said, looking around the room. I didn't see any stairs. "How do I get up there?"

"See that?" Frank pointed at the far corner, where a big steel cabinet lay on its side. Planted atop the fallen cabinet was a small refrigerator, and in the ceiling right above the refrigerator was a hole about half the size of a tatami mat. Probably where the stairs had been ripped out.

"You can climb up to the second floor from the refrigerator," he said, smiling at me. "Lots of beds up there. It's like a hotel."

All he'd have to do was move the refrigerator after I climbed up, and there'd be no need to watch me all night. It would take guts to leap down from that hole in the ceiling. The floor was covered with shards of glass from the toppled cabinet, and jumping down would result in a lot of noise and possibly a broken leg or two.

"This must've been a hospital," Frank said as I scanned the room. "I found it while I was taking a walk. Pretty good hideout, don't you think? No running water, but there's electricity, so instead of showering I just heat up some mineral water in my coffee maker and wash with that. All the comforts of home."

Along with the water, the gas and electricity would surely be turned off in a ruin like this. I wondered where he was stealing electricity from but didn't ask. Something like that would be child's play for Frank.

"Why do they ring the bells a hundred and eight times? The Lebanese fellow had this really fascinating explanation but she couldn't remember all of it. Anyway, after having that beautiful experience with the bells she started studying about Japan, and I'll tell you, she knows more about this place than anybody I ever met. Like those girls in the pub? They didn't know anything about their own country. Not only did they not know anything, they didn't even seem to be interested. All they cared about was expensive bourbon and clothes and handbags and hotels and things. That amazed me—them knowing nothing at all about their own history."

They couldn't learn about it now even if they wanted to, I thought to myself. A picture of Frank cutting Lady #5's throat threatened to form in my mind, and the fear came back, just like before, when he'd suddenly appeared behind me on the street. My spine felt funny, all the strength drained from my legs, and a mold-like odor filled my nostrils and then spread from the nasal passages throughout my body, the smell sticking like a coat of paint to the underside of my skin. But the image of Lady #5's slit throat didn't materialize. I'd received warning that a nauseating image was going to appear on my mental screen, and then the screen had gone blank. It was hard to believe, but I was beginning to forget the actual scene of the massacre. I tried to visualize Mr. Children's ear being lopped off but couldn't. I remembered it as a factual event, but the image of it had faded. Sometimes you can remember everything about an old friend, down to minor details about his behavior, but for the life of you you can't picture his face. Or you'll wake up knowing you've just had a terrifying dream but can't remember what it was about. It was like that. Why that sort of thing happens I couldn't tell you, but there it was.

"Meanwhile, here's this Peruvian hooker who knows all kinds of fascinating things about Japanese history. For example, from way back—thousands of years ago—the Japanese just focused on growing rice, and even when things started coming in from overseas, like the *taiko* drum and metals from Persia, the rice-farming traditions didn't change. But as soon as the Portuguese brought rifles, everything changed, and the Japanese started having wars all the time. Previously they'd only fought with swords—I've seen that in movies, it looks like ballet, almost. But warfare with guns increased year by year, and the Japanese started invading other countries, and because they hadn't had much experience with foreigners they were incompetent at occupying a country or relating to its citizens, so people in the neighboring countries grew to hate them. This misguided sort of warfare continued right up until the A-bombs fell. And then, after that, Japan changed its way of thinking and gave up war and started making electric appliances and became an economic superpower, so obviously that was the path the country should have followed all along. They lost the war, but it was a war over vested interests in China and Southeast Asia, so now after all these years you might say Japan won it after all. But why do they ring the bells a hundred and eight times, Kenji? Can you tell me? She only had a rough idea."

I thought maybe Frank was testing me. To see if I was knowledgeable enough to serve as his guide to the New Year's bells. What would happen if I failed the test?

I said: "In Buddhism . . ." *Or was it Shinto?* I thought—but Frank wouldn't know the difference. "In Buddhism, what you're calling 'bad instincts' are known as *bonno*. Bon-no, with two ens, like 'bone' and 'no.' But the meaning is a lot deeper than 'bad instincts.' "

Frank was fascinated by the sound of the word and practiced pronouncing it: Bon-no, bon-no. . . .

"Gosh," he sighed. "What an amazing word. Just saying it makes me feel like something is melting away inside, or like I'm being wrapped in a soft, warm blanket. Bon-no . . . What exactly does it mean, Kenji?"

"I think it's usually translated as 'worldly desires.' It's more complicated than that, but the first thing you need to know is that it's something everybody suffers from."

I was surprised to hear myself saying these things, because I didn't know I knew them. I couldn't remember being taught this or reading it somewhere. I couldn't even remember the last time I'd heard the word "bonno" pronounced. But I knew what it meant and even the usual English translation. When I told Frank that everybody suffered from it he looked, believe it or not, as if he was going to cry.

"Kenji," he said with a little quaver in his voice, "please, tell me more."

I did, wondering all the while where and when I'd picked up this information. It was like having data sleeping away on your hard disk and then stumbling across software that unlocks it.

"There's another word, *madou*, which means, like, to lose your way." I told him to think of "Ma" as in mother, and "dough" as in bread, and he began practicing the pronunciation. Old Japanese words like this sound even more solemn and mysterious when spoken by foreigners.

"Madou is the simplest verb for expressing what bonno are, or what they do to you. Bonno make you lose your way. 'Bad instincts' makes them sound like something you're born with, something you need to be punished for, which isn't quite right. There are six categories of bonno, or sometimes ten—or sometimes just two big categories. They're kind of like the Seven Deadly Sins in Christianity, but the difference is that *everybody* suffers from them. They're as much a part of being human as, like, our vital organs are. But the six categories, or ten or whatever, are all things I can't translate into English, so it's hard to explain."

Frank nodded and said he understood. "It must be hard to translate such deep words into a simple language like English."

"The two basic categories of bonno are the ones that come from thoughts and the ones that come from feelings. The ones you get from thoughts might disappear if someone just points out the truth to you. But the ones you get from feelings are more difficult. To wash those away you have to train very hard. Have you ever heard how Buddhists go without eating, or swim naked in icy water, or stand under waterfalls in winter, or sit crosslegged in this unnatural position and get smacked from behind with sticks?"

Frank said yeah, he'd seen documentaries like that on TV.

"But Buddhism has a lot of very sweet, gentle things about it too," I told him. "Like the New Year's bells. If you keep dividing up all the different bonno into smaller and smaller categories, you end up with a hundred and eight worldly desires. So they ring the bells that many times to free the listeners from each one."

Frank asked where the best place to listen to the bells was. And that's when I remembered how I'd learned about all this stuff. When Jun had been so angry at me for breaking our Christmas date, I'd promised her that we'd spend New Year's Eve together. In order to decide what to do that night we'd bought and looked through several city guides—*Pia* and *Tokyo Walker* and so on. I forget which magazine it was, but one of them had a section titled something like "Joya-no-kane: Know the Traditions to Enjoy Them More!" and I'd read it aloud to her.

"The Peruvian woman said it was incredibly crowded, I mean the place she went to listen to the bells, and she wished she could have heard them in a quieter place. Kenji, do you know a nice quiet temple we can go to? I'm not comfortable in big crowds."

The thought of trudging through Meiji Shrine with Frank and hundreds of thousands of other people didn't appeal much to me, either. I told him I knew a good place.

"It's a bridge."

Frank gave me a baffled look.

"A bridge?"

One of the magazines had mentioned it, and Jun and I had decided that was where we'd go to hear the ringing of the bells. It was a bridge over the Sumida River, but I couldn't remember the name. I looked at my watch. Three A.M., December 31. I wondered if Jun was still up.

"Kenji, what do you mean, a bridge? I don't understand."

There weren't many temples in this area, around Shinjuku, I told him. "The Shitamachi district—downtown?—has far more of them. But like the Peruvian woman said, thousands and thousands of people pack into those temples—they're the *least* peaceful places on New Year's Eve. But if you stand on this bridge, you can hear the sound of the bells echoing off the steel. They say it's amazing."

I saw something flicker in Frank's sunken and normally expressionless eyes. Deep inside them a tiny light came on.

"That's where I want to go, then," he said, the underside of his chin quivering. "Take me there, Kenji. Please."

I told him my girlfriend knew the name of the bridge, and got out my phone to call Jun. As I was dialing I realized for the first time how very cold it was in here. My fingers were so numb I accidentally pressed the wrong numbers several times before getting it right.

"Is that you, Kenji?" Jun answered on the first ring. I pictured her sitting up with her mobile, waiting for me to call. She must be worried.

"Yeah, it's me," I said as calmly as possible. But whether from the cold or from the tension, my voice was shaking again. At least I was aware of it this time.

"Where are you? Back in your apartment?"

"I'm still with Frank."

"Where?"

"At his hotel."

"The Hilton?"

"Not the Hilton, no, it's a smaller place. A little business hotel. I don't know the name exactly, but it's nice."

I had an idea. I didn't know if it was a good one. I was cold and sleepy and emotionally exhausted, and maybe it was a terrible idea, but it was the only one I had. The mouthpiece was frosting up with my breath. Frank was staring at me, and the fluorescent lamp on the floor made his face an unearthly blue and strangely warped. At least he won't kill me, I thought. Not till I've taken him to that bridge, anyway.

"Jun, we're going out to hear Joya-no-kane tonight, me and Frank. I have to guide him there."

"Very funny."

"No, really. It's what we decided."

"Oh?"

She sounded angry. I was breaking my promise again, and any concern about me had shifted to the back burner now. But I needed her to be at that bridge. My plan, such as it was, was to have Jun keep an eye on us. She could probably even have arranged for Frank to be arrested, but that would require a long explanation about what had happened in the omiai pub. And if I told her the whole story, I was sure she'd freak out—if she even believed me, that is. Besides, the killing scene was already fading from my memory. And I didn't want to be grilled endlessly by the police and forced to quit working as a guide, I was sure of that now. *Jun, he really is the killer, go to the police, have them come with you*—I just couldn't bring myself to say that. It would be asking for trouble.

"What was the name of that bridge?" I said.

"What bridge?"

She was pissed off all right. When I'd canceled our plan for Christmas dinner at a fancy hotel because I had to work, she was furious and said something to the effect that the only reason she even bothered to have a boyfriend was so she could spend Christmas with him. Christmas has a special importance for high-school girls. Jun and her friends don't really need guys—boyfriends, I mean. I've often heard them say that boyfriends are more trouble than they're worth, that most boys don't have anything interesting to say, or any money either. And in fact Jun had spent more time with her friends during the past summer, going to the beach and whatnot, than with me. But Christmas is a special ritual for them, the one precious night of the year to spend some real quality time with a guy. I had denied her that, and now I was saying I'd be with Frank on New Year's Eve. I couldn't blame her for being angry.

"You know. The bridge in the magazine, where the sound of the bells is supposed to echo off the girders? Over the Sumida River. What was the name of it again?"

"I forget," she said. "Sorry." Translation: Figure it out for yourself, jerk.

"Jun, this is important. Look, I don't want to worry you, but—how can I put this? My life may depend on it."

I heard a gasp, then a frantic jumble of words. Hang on, I told her, cutting in. Frank was gazing at me with his cow face.

"Keep calm, okay? Please just listen carefully to what I'm about to say. It's not a joke, and I'm not just making it up. And when I'm done, no questions, okay? I don't have time to explain everything. That's just the way it is right now. Are you with me?"

"Yes," she said in a hoarse whisper.

"Good. First of all, can you try to remember the name of that bridge?"

"Kachidoki," she said. I knew she hadn't forgotten it. "It's out by the fish market, near Tsukiji." I could hear the tension in her voice. "The next one downriver from Tsukuda Bridge."

"Go there tonight," I told her. "But don't come up to us. I just want you to keep an eye on Frank and me."

"Keep an eye on you? What do you mean?"

There was no way to make it all perfectly clear. I had to stick just to the essentials.

"Tonight, by ten o'clock at the very latest, Frank and I will be at the foot of Kachidoki Bridge, on the fish market side. I'll make sure that's where we are—the foot of Kachidoki Bridge, ten o'clock. Got it?"

"Wait a minute, Kenji."

"What."

"Sorry. What do you mean 'the foot'?"

"Where the bridge, you know, begins."

"Got it."

"Look for me and Frank, but don't show yourself. When you see us, just pretend you don't know who we are. Whatever you do, don't come up to us or talk to us. Understood?"

"So I'm just supposed to watch you from a distance, right?"

"Exactly. When the last bell has been struck, Frank and I will split up, and I'll go back home with you. If Frank tries to stop me, or if I seem to be struggling with him—if that happens, and only if that happens, find a policeman and get him to step in and help me. Okay? There are bound to be a lot of cops around to control the crowds. I intend to walk away from Frank after the last bell, no matter what. If I don't, it means Frank is pulling something, so do whatever you have to do, start screaming or whatever, to get a cop to help me get away from him. Don't try to do anything on your own, that's very important, get a policeman or two. You understand me?"

"I understand."

"All right. I have to go now. See you tonight."

"Kenji, wait. Can I ask just one more question?"

"What?"

"So Frank is a bad guy after all?"

"Pretty bad, yeah," I said and switched off the phone.

I told Frank I'd found out the name of the bridge, but that when the bells were done ringing I wanted him to let me go. I was amazed at how calmly I was able to say this. I guess I felt I'd done all I could do. To have Jun watch the two of us—that was all my creative resources were up to. No matter how long I sweated over the problem, it wasn't likely I'd come up with anything better.

"I don't like cops very much in the first place, and if I went to them they'd make me stop working as a guide. Besides, I don't even know your family name. I'm not going to tell the police anything, Frank. So when the bells stop ringing, I want you to let me go. Okay?"

"Of course," said Frank. "That's what I planned to do from the beginning, you don't need to ask your girlfriend to do anything. Haven't I been saying all along that I consider you my friend?"

I looked at Frank, thinking: It's only been about thirty hours since I first met this guy. It seemed like his voice and manner of speaking had reverted to the way they were then, in the cafeteria of that hotel. Of course, that was no reason to trust anything he said. With somebody like Frank, even if he did regard me as a friend, it didn't necessarily mean he wouldn't murder me.

"Sleepy, Kenji?"

I shook my head. A few minutes ago I would have been happy to stretch out even on the broken glass on the floor, but, maybe because of that intense conversation with Jun, my drowsiness had vanished. Frank looked like he was about to say something but hesitated. He opened his mouth to speak, then stopped himself again. Finally he got up and fetched a bottle of Evian water from the refrigerator. He took a sip and asked if I wanted anything, and I said I'd have a cola. The refrigerator was one of those small, squat, old-fashioned jobs, probably salvaged from someone's trash, but I could see it was well stocked with soft drinks and even beer.

"I want to tell you something, Kenji. It's a long story, and pretty strange, too, but I'd like for you to hear it, if you don't mind."

Frank was speaking in what was, for him, a meek-sounding voice. I'm listening, I said.

"I grew up in a plain little town on the East Coast, you wouldn't know the name, in a plain little house like you see in old American movies, with a small lawn and a front porch just made for an old lady in a rocking chair."

Frank's voice and even the expression on his face had grown more relaxed and tranquil since we'd entered this ruined building. What kind of neighborhood was this, anyway? It was packed with small apartment buildings, and yet not a sound was to be heard from anywhere outside. The bare fluorescent unit on the floor emitted a faint electric buzz, and the refrigerator made a vague, high-pitched whine, like tinnitus. That was all I could hear, though. The broken windows and collapsed walls were covered with those vinyl sheets and canvas dropcloths, but we had no heat and it was freezing. My breath made little white clouds. Frank's didn't.

"We moved there when I was seven years old, because in the town before that I had already killed two people."

My ears pricked up at the word "killed," and I found myself asking: "How old?"

"I was . . . seven," Frank said slowly and took a sip of Evian. Unbelievable, I mumbled—and it felt like an unbelievably stupid thing to say. I'd been expecting just another of Frank's lies, but somehow the words "seven years old" sucked me right in.

"The town I was born in had a population of maybe eight thousand. An old historical port town with what they claimed was the fourth oldest golf course in America, not a championship course or anything but famous enough that people would fly in from New York and Washington just to play it. We weren't far from Portland, where they had an airport, and just a short drive from Canada, too. People in that part of Canada spoke French, so it really seemed like a foreign country, and that thrilled me as a kid. The town had once had streetcars, which was unusual for a town of that size, and even though they'd stopped running before I was born, the tracks were still there. I used to love those tracks, the steel rails buried in the road. I liked to play a game where I would walk along them as far as I could go. I thought they must go on forever, because no matter how far I went the rails never seemed to end. I honestly believed that if you kept following them you'd eventually see the entire world. But what I remember most about those times was getting lost. Did you ever get lost when you were a kid, Kenji?"

I shook my head.

"That's funny," said Frank. "All kids get lost."

I did remember my father lecturing me about that when I was very small. He told me many times that whenever children play by themselves they end up getting lost. So always play with others, Kenji, never play outside alone, or a bad man might come and snatch you away!

As this memory of my father was unreeling, I was startled to hear Frank use the word "Daddy."

"Daddy used to say that it was as if I'd learned to walk just in order to get lost, because that's what I started doing almost as soon as I could toddle around."

I guess when he said he'd killed people by the time he was seven I somehow pictured Little Frank as an orphan. I once read a novel like that, about a kid who lost his parents and grew up in an old-folks home his grandmother ran and turned into a serial killer. "Is your father still alive?" I blurted out. "Daddy?" Frank muttered with a rueful smile. "He's still around somewhere, I guess," he said, staring down at the floor.

"I remember very clearly what it was like getting lost," he went on. "The circumstances varied, but the moment I realized I was lost was always the same. No kid ever got lost gradually. Suddenly you find yourself in unfamiliar surroundings, and that's it, you're lost. You've been walking along past familiar houses and parks and streets, and then you turn a corner and the scenery changes completely. I remember being very scared when that happened but also really liking it. A lot of times I'd get lost following somebody. It started as soon as I was able to walk around outside, so how old could I have been? Three or so, I guess. The ones I followed most were the men in the fire brigade's brass band. The local firehouse was right near my home, and the brass band was famous in those parts for winning contests, and they practiced a lot, marching around as they played. I used to follow their little parades, but you can't walk that fast at three, so I'd fall behind. The sousaphones and tubas always brought up the rear of the parade, and I remember how it felt watching those big, shiny horns march away into the distance. It was like the world was leaving me behind, and then I'd look around and realize I was lost. One day when that happened, Mama was driving home from the grocery store and saw me walking along the street."

The word "Mama" seemed to come as naturally to Frank as "Daddy" had. But I didn't ask if she was still alive. Something told me I shouldn't.

"I remember exactly how I felt right then, but how to describe it? It was the same atmosphere as always when I got lost. I only knew the geography around my house, the immediate neighborhood. That was the whole world to me, and it was T-shaped, if you see what I mean, because it consisted of the street that ran in front of our house and the little road that started right across the street and narrowed down to nothing in the distance. I even remember the edges of my world, where the borders were marked. To the left was a neighbor's blue mailbox, to the right, at the corner of the street, was a flowering dogwood tree, and straight ahead, down that sloping little road, was a steel bench in a park with a brook running through it. Those were the edges of the world—a mailbox, a dogwood tree, and a park bench—and the moment I stepped beyond any of them I was outside my world and lost. Even though I did it over and over again and must have seen the scenery plenty of times before, I could never familiarize myself with the landscape out there beyond the borders, in the Unknown, which is what it was for me, like the dark forests were for people in the Middle Ages. The day I ran into Mama was a cloudy day in late spring, early summer. That part of the East Coast is cloudy a lot, with so much humidity it's almost like a mist in the air, blocking out the sun. Muggy, but when the wind blows it feels chilly on your skin. A lot of people there develop asthma or bronchial problems, and I seem to remember the adults coughing all the time. On this particular day I'd ventured into the Unknown beyond the blue mailbox. When you're a kid, getting lost isn't just an event or a situation, it's like a career move. You get this thrill of anxiety and fear and a feeling that you've done something that can never be undone. My sense of myself, of my body, would become very shaky, and I'd feel like I was going to melt into the gray fog all around me. A lot of times I'd start screaming. But adults never pay any attention to a little kid alone on the street just screaming—crying, maybe, but not screaming. On this day I was mostly just afraid but still really excited. And then

Mama appeared. All of a sudden she pulled up beside me in the car and said: 'Goodness, it's my little boy!' I started bawling, not because I was happy or relieved to see her but because I was scared. I felt like Mama had merged with the Unknown and must therefore be a completely different person. I thought I somehow had to find a way back to the world I knew, and when Mama went to take me in her arms I shook her off and tried to run away. I wasn't supposed to meet up with Mama here, I was only supposed to see her back in the real world, and so this woman couldn't be my real Mama even though she looked just like her. So when she grabbed me again I bit her on the wrist, so hard that my jaw went numb. I didn't think I had any choice, I didn't know what else to do. Mama was yelling her head off. I guess I bit right through the skin where there was an artery or something, because blood started gushing out into my mouth, lots of it, and I was biting so hard I couldn't breathe, so I gulped it all down, like a baby nursing at its mother's breast, just sucking up the blood. I felt like I had to, like if I didn't drink it all up I'd suffocate. Have you ever swallowed somebody else's blood, Kenji?"

I was too nauseated to reply. After two years of working as a guide and interpreter, I'd finally got to the point where I could think in English—I mean, go straight from the English words to the pictures they evoked. Until then, I'd had to translate everything in my head first. For example, if somebody said "blood" I would first have to change it to *chi* in my mind, and only then could I picture what it meant. But the English verb "swallow" and the noun "blood" were all it took to form a picture in my brain, and now Frank was asking me, in a perfectly casual way, if I'd ever done the thing my poor brain was picturing. He wasn't talking in a spooky voice, like the narrator in a horror film or something: *Are you ready for something reeeally scary? When's the last time you tasted hot, red, dripping blood? Bwah, ha ha ha!* It was nothing like that. It was more like the tone of voice you might use to ask someone if they'd ever ridden a horse. Ever swallow someone's blood? I looked down at the floor and slowly shook my head.

"For me, that was the first time, my own Mama's blood," Frank said gloomily. "The blood itself is no big deal—not particularly good-tasting or bitter or sweet or anything—so it's not as if you get addicted to the flavor."

I sat with my chin down, hugging my knees, nodding from time to time as he talked. The fluorescent lamp cast its light upward in an inverted pyramid, leaving the floor and the mattress we were sitting on in darkness. Now that my eyes were used to the dim light down there I could see that the floor was covered with a thick layer of dust and alive with bugs. The bugs were of a sort I didn't recognize, and they congregated at these dark patches that stained the floorboards here and there. I figured Frank had killed somebody in this ruined clinic. Or killed them somewhere else, then brought the body here to cut it up with some of the medical equipment scattered around. Maybe this was where he'd found the long, thin knife he used in the omiai pub.

"After I bit Mama that time, my parents took me to a child psychologist, and he came to the conclusion that because I hadn't nursed much as a baby I had a chronic calcium deficiency that made me emotionally unstable, and also that the splatter films my older brothers took me to had been a bad influence. They didn't use the term 'splatter film' in those days, but both of my brothers, who were quite a bit older than me, loved horror movies, as about ninety-nine percent of American kids do. Later, after I killed those two people, the police found a lot of gory film clips and posters and rubber masks and things at our house, and the media decided that was what had made me do it, the influence of horror movies. They needed a reason why a little kid would commit murder, someone or something to point the finger at, and I think they were relieved when they hit upon horror movies as the culprit. But there's no *reason* a child commits murder, just as there's no reason a child gets lost. What would it be—because his parents weren't watching him? That's not a reason, it's just a step in the process."

It was almost 4:00 A.M. now, and the cold was getting harder and harder to bear. Frank didn't seem to notice it, though. I had my overcoat on, but he was wearing only a thin sweater and corduroy jacket. In two nights with Frank,

I'd yet to catch him showing any real sign of being cold. He saw me cupping my hands together and blowing on them for warmth and said: "Chilly?" I nodded, and to my surprise he took off his own jacket and tried to drape it over my shoulders. "No, you need that!" I said, pulling away. Frank told me it was okay, he never got cold, and pushed up his sleeves to show me his wrists. Just as I'd noticed in the omiai pub, they were ribbed with countless suicide scars. I wondered what, if anything, the scars had to do with not getting cold.

"After that first time, I became obsessed with the thought that I might do it again, drink somebody else's blood, not because I liked the taste of it but because I was haunted by the act itself, because it's extreme and abnormal but imaginable. Human beings are the only creatures who have the power of imagination, and that's why we survived. Physically we were no match for other large animals, so certain things were needed to keep out of danger, like the ability to conceptualize and predict and communicate and confirm, all of which are possible only because of the power of imagination. Our ancestors were capable of imagining all kinds of horrors, which they had to try to prevent from becoming realities. And modern people still have the same ability. When it's used in positive ways you get artists and scientists and so on, but when it's used in negative ways it always turns into fear and anxiety and hatred, and it can cause a lot of damage. People often point out how cruel children can be, because they'll torture or kill little animals and insects or smash their own toys. But kids don't do things like that for fun, they do it to release the anxieties of the imagination out into the real world. If they can't bear the thought of torturing or killing bugs, they feel an unconscious urge to actually do it and reassure themselves that the world won't come tumbling down. In my case, I couldn't bear the stress of imagining I might lap up somebody's blood again, so when I was four I slashed my wrists. That was the first time I'd ever really tried to hurt myself. Everybody flipped out, and they took me to a shrink again, but again he just told them not to let me watch horror movies. It's true I was fond of that sort of movie but not to the extent my brothers were. Basically people who love horror movies are people with boring lives. They want to be stimulated, and they need to reassure themselves, because when a really scary movie is over, you're reassured to see that you're still alive and the world still exists as it did before. That's the real reason we have horror films—they act as shock absorbers—and if they disappeared altogether it would mean losing one of the few ways we have to ease the anxiety of the imagination. And I bet you'd see a big leap in the number of serial killers and mass murderers. After all, anyone stupid enough to get the idea of murdering people from a movie could get the same idea from watching the news, right? From the age of four to six I cut my wrists about a dozen times, and I'll tell you something, Kenji, you don't know what cold is until you've experienced the cold you feel when the blood is draining out of your body. My parents finally hired somebody to watch me, this ugly woman, and eventually she caught me trying to cut my own throat and beat the living hell out of me. So one evening in autumn while she was in the bathroom I stuffed my brother's hunting knife in the waistband of my pants, pocketed some madeleines Mama had baked that morning, and left the house and got lost for the first time in a long, long time. I just marched on up the street, and when I came to those good old streetcar tracks, I remembered how I used to walk along them when I was smaller. The street was asphalt mixed with crushed seashells and had the rusty old rails half-buried in it. The bits of seashell were pretty, the way they glittered in the setting sun, and I just kept walking on up the hill. I'd done that many, many times before, set out for the top of the hill, but had always stopped halfway up. The street started getting narrower, and I was already lost of course, but I never stopped to look back. I was afraid that if I did, I might find that everything was gone, because I had this feeling that one or the other of the two worlds was going to disappear. So I made up my mind not to look behind me and forged ahead. The knife was so heavy it was hard to keep it from slipping down my pants. I pressed my hand against it and walked along just staring down at my feet and the rusty rails and the seashells in the asphalt, and then suddenly the rails stopped. This shocked me to the core, because I'd always thought they never ended. I remember standing there for a really long time staring down at the spot where they stopped, thinking this must be the actual edge of the world. And then I looked up and realized I was at the top of the hill. In front of me was a pond, and when I turned to look back I could see the whole town laid out below in miniature, like a diorama. I'd never seen this view because I'd never made it to the top before, but there it was, the whole town, with clusters of houses and shops on the slopes of the valley, and in the center were bigger buildings and churches and parks, and from there to the harbor were the factories with their smokestacks and warehouses, and the giant crane at the shipyard, which I recognized from one time when my brother took me there, but which now looked like a toy. Beyond that was the sea, gray and hazy, and I could smell the salt in the wind, and behind me the sun was a huge ball sitting on the horizon, and I felt this overwhelming sense of power, and at the same time this extreme panic and anxiety. It was as if the whole world was bowing down at my feet, but also as if I alone was cut off from the world, and I just stood there thinking, *Holy moly*. I was overwhelmed. It was like receiving a revelation from God. At the top of the hill was an old, abandoned, open-pit coal mine, and the long, winding trenches had filled with water to form the pond. Dozens of swans were there, migrating from their summer home in Quebec or somewhere, and I walked around the edge of the pond, where all these reeds were growing, and found a big rock and sat down on it and took the madeleines out of my pocket and crumbled them up and threw little pieces into the pond. I didn't know if swans would eat madeleines or not, but they came gliding over the water toward me, a whole flock of them. I knew that if I reached out to them they'd back off, because I was like that myself in those days—if somebody or something came at me with no warning, I always assumed they were the enemy and ran away. One swan came right up near me, a young one that wasn't as wary as the others yet. I still remember the graceful curve of its neck, and how its white feathers were tinged with orange from the setting sun, and my heart was pounding so hard I thought it was going to knock my teeth out. I had to keep telling myself: Not yet, not yet. The swan swam into the reeds beside me, to where I could have reached out and touched its long, slender throat, but I still just sat there not moving except to flick crumbs into the water with my fingers. And then I pulled the knife from my waistband, very slowly and quietly, and removed it from its leather sheath. It was heavy and really sharp, my brother's knife, and I thought: This will put everything right. I thought it would reconcile my sense that I was cut off from the world with my sense that the world was at my feet, make those two feelings merge into one inside me. The swan was just inches away from my rock when I slowly raised the knife, rested the blade on my shoulder, and then in one quick motion slashed down at the base of its neck with all my might. I didn't know there were bones in a swan's neck, but I heard the sound, like a dry twig snapping. The knife went right through, and blood came gushing out. It wasn't like Mama's blood, it had a sweet taste, and at the time I thought it must be because of the madeleines. I drank an awful lot of it, more than you'd think would be in a bird that size. Nobody ever found out I'd killed the swan, though, because the coal mine was a place where a lot of bad things had happened, rape and things, and people almost never went up there."

Frank stopped for a minute, bowed his head, and covered his eyes with his hands. I thought for a moment he was crying, but he wasn't. His eyes hurt, he said softly.

"I haven't slept, and when I don't sleep for a long time my eyes get tired. All the rest of me is fine—but my eyes, they really hurt."

I asked him how long he'd gone without sleep. About a hundred and twenty hours, he said. A hundred and twenty hours added up to five whole days. I wondered if he was taking speed or something. I have friends who are hooked on speed. Jun says there are girls in her class who are, too. Speed freaks can go for days without sleeping. I asked Frank if he took drugs, but he shook his head.

"Later, in the same town, the town I was born in, I killed two people, and when the police questioned me they decided I was insane, so they put me in this mental hospital that I believe was run by the military. The feeling that the world was at my feet and the feeling that I alone was cut off from the world, the sense of power and the anxiety, had both stayed with me ever since that evening at the pond. In the hospital they gave me a ton of medicine, mixed up in my food. They had me on a liquid diet and fed me through a tube, a plastic tube with a little knob at the end made of silicone, which they'd force deep down my throat. I guess it was designed for people with throat cancer or something, who couldn't swallow. Ingenious design. But they fed me way too much, and that, along with the side effects of the medicine, made me fatter and fatter, until my face got all pale and bloated, and it began to feel like this body wasn't even me, like I was stuffed with feathers, or just liquid, a liquefied human being. That was with me for years—feeling I wasn't myself. And I do think I wasn't my real self then. Of course, I'm not sure there is such a thing as a real self. You could ransack your innards looking for the real you and never find it—slice yourself open and all you'll find is blood and muscle and bone. . . . A year later I was released from the hospital fat as a pig, a physical wreck. My family had moved to this little town in Virginia, and they came and got me, but from that point on Daddy and my brothers hardly ever said two words to me. About ten years later, when I went to prison as an adult, my oldest brother came to visit and explained about those days. He said they hadn't known how to relate to me or what to talk about, not because I'd killed people but because I was so fat I looked like a complete stranger. I first started going without much sleep, just taking naps sometimes, when I was in the mental hospital for the fourth time and they cut out part of my brain. I was fifteen. In the operation, they open a small hole in your skull and insert an instrument like an ice pick into the white matter and sever the nerve fibers, which usually makes you very quiet and docile. Americans love to mess about with the brain—that's why they're at the forefront of neurosurgery. I was already into black magic by then, and I'd met a lot of people in the hospitals and reform schools who taught me things like how to cut someone's throat without spraying blood around and where exactly to slice somebody's Achilles tendon so it'll make a high-pitched twang —useful stuff like that—and I learned hypnosis too, which came so easily to me I couldn't believe it. I'm not saying I feel *fulfilled* when I kill people. When it's happening I often think there must be something else I should be doing, and sometimes I feel like I'm right on the verge of discovering what that something else might be, because the interesting thing is, when I'm killing, that's when I'm the most focused on life, the most clearheaded, but . . . Have you ever been in a mental hospital, Kenji?"

The things he was talking about were fundamentally creepy and disgusting, and a lot of what he said made no sense to me, but it was all sinking in. It was like listening to music, rhythmical and with a sort of melody that seemed to get inside me directly, through my pores rather than my ears. I'd surrendered to his storytelling, I guess, and when he asked if I'd ever been in a mental hospital it didn't even strike me as an outrageous question. I just said no, I hadn't. Listening to him, I'd ceased to think of Frank as insane or not insane. I felt like someone listening to an ancient myth: *Long, long ago, when men used to kill and eat one another* . . . I wasn't sure I knew any longer what was right and what was wrong. It was a very precarious feeling, but it hinted at a sense of liberation like I'd never experienced. Liberation from the countless little hassles of everyday life. It was as if the border between "me" and "not me" was dissolving, leaving me in a sort of slush.

I was going somewhere I'd never been before.

"Mental hospitals are interesting places," Frank said. "I'll never forget hearing about this experiment they did with cats. They put the cat in a cage that has a button in the floor, and when he steps on the button he gets food, so after a while he learns to do that, press the button when he wants food, and then they take him away and starve him for a while and then put him back in the same cage with the same button, only this time when he steps on it he gets a shock. Not a big shock, just a mild current, but the result's the same. The cat becomes unbalanced, completely neurotic, and in the end he loses the will to eat, even refuses food when it's offered to him, and starves to death. The man who told me this was a specialist in psychological testing. You know anything about psychological tests, Kenji? I've taken hundreds of them. The most famous one is probably the Minnesota Multiphasic Personality Inventory, but I took so many that eventually I memorized all the different types of questions, and by the time I was in my late teens I was more familiar with the tests than the people testing me were. Would you like to try one?"

The story of the experiment really spoke to me. First the cat learns something, and it's fun for him because he's rewarded with food, but then they starve him and reward the learned behavior with pain. Naturally the cat doesn't understand what the hell's going on. I experienced things like that nearly every day when I was a kid. I don't mean big things like my father's death, just ordinary everyday dilemmas and double binds. You can't change the grownup world to suit your idea of how things should be, so you have to learn to press the right buttons, and kids growing up find themselves constantly in situations just like that cat's. There's no consistency to the way your parents and other adults respond to you when you're a kid. It's especially inconsistent in this country, because there aren't any solid, standard criteria for judging what's important. The grownups live only for money and things with established monetary value, like designer goods. The media—TV, newspapers, magazines, radio, whatever—are full of pronouncements by adults that make it clear that all they really want or care about is money and material goods. From politicians and bureaucrats to the lowliest office drudge drinking cheap saké at some outdoor stall, they all show by the way they live that money is the only thing they aspire to. They'll puff themselves up and say "Money isn't everything," but all you have to do is watch their behavior to see where their real priorities lie. The weeklies that cater to middle-aged men criticize compensated dating among high-school girls, but in the same issue you'll find recommendations for reasonably priced erotic massage parlors and early morning soaplands. They'll denounce the corruption amongst politicians and bureaucrats but also feature "can't-miss" stock tips and "bargain" real-estate deals. And they'll do entire photo spreads on "success stories," showing us rich people's houses or some asshole standing there in designer clothes and accessories. Pretty much all day long, day in and day out, three hundred sixty-five days a year, children in this country go through what that food-or-electric-shock cat went through. But try to point that out, and some old fucker will jump all over you. *You kids are spoiled rotten! How dare you complain, when you've never lacked for anything in your life? Why, my generation lived on potatoes and worked our fingers to the bone to make this the wealthy country it is!* It's always precisely the sort of smug old wanker you would never *ever* want to end up like. We don't live the way you tell us to because we're afraid that if we do we'll grow up to be like you, and the thought of that is unbearable. It's all right for you because you'll be dead soon anyway, but we've still got another fifty or sixty years to live in this stinking country.

"Kenji, what's wrong?"

Frank was staring at me. "Nothing," I said. He took a sip of Evian and smiled: "You look angry." That story about the cat was interesting, I told him, taking a sip of my Coke. I had left the can on the floor beside me, and it was still ice-cold. What a weird place this was, I thought. It felt completely isolated and, partly because of the cold, like being on another planet. I wondered if there were planets where it's okay to murder people. I decided there must be, reminding myself that in war, after all, killers are heroes. And it suddenly occurred to me why I hadn't run to that police box in Kabuki-cho. The victims in the omiai pub, when placed in the position of the cat with the button, hadn't put up any resistance. I looked over at Frank and thought: Well, here's a guy who resisted. Maybe he was one of the very few who'd kicked against this cat's cage of a world, where first they feed you and then, although you've committed no crime, they give you a punishing jolt. Looking at Frank, lit from below by the lamp, I began to think of him as a man who'd been stepped on all his life but never caved in.

"Let's try a little psychological test," he said, and started asking me some of the questions he'd memorized. Well, not questions exactly, more like statements to which I had to answer "true" or "false." He told me I had to answer at once, without thinking. The statements were of all sorts, from "I like poems about flowers" to "My genitals are oddly shaped" and "My greatest pleasure is to be hurt by someone I love." Over the course of half an hour or so he must have rattled off over two hundred of them.

"Interesting, isn't it?" Frank smiled when we were done. "I put them together myself. Like I say, I've taken hundreds of these tests. In fact, I'd say I'm one of the world's foremost authorities on psychological testing."

"Is there anything wrong with me?" I asked. "I mean, according to the test?"

"Don't worry, Kenji, you're normal. You exhibit a certain amount of confusion, a few contradictory impulses, but that's true of all mentally normal people. It's the ones who're rigid in their likes and dislikes who are in trouble. Everybody lives with a certain amount of confusion and indecision—never knowing which way the pendulum's going to swing. That's normal."

What about him? I asked, and Frank said he was normal too. This didn't even strike me as peculiar. I thought he probably was.

Starting with that piece of human skin plastered to my door, today had been just one unimaginable thing after another. But though I knew I was exhausted, I was too wired to be able to sleep. Besides, it was freezing cold, and I was sitting with a murderer in an abandoned building littered with medical junk. I think all of these things contributed to my mental state being slightly out of whack. It wasn't that Frank was exerting an evil influence on me, winning me over to the Dark Side or whatever. But I can't deny that my body and mind were being dragged into unfamiliar territory. I felt like I was listening to the tales of a guide in some unexplored country.

"You must be tired," Frank said. "There are still plenty of things I haven't told you, but I guess we'd better call it a day. Tonight we have to go hear the bells and everything."

"I don't think I can sleep."

"Why not? You afraid I'll kill you?"

"No. It's just that my nerves are kind of on edge."

"Maybe you should eat something."

I wasn't hungry, I told him, but Frank said I'd sleep better if I had something in my stomach. He took a coffee maker from one of the cardboard boxes stacked against the wall, filled it with Evian, and plugged it in. Then he took two cups of King Ra instant ramen from the same box. I asked if he always ate instant foods. Sure, he said with a grin.

"I'm no gourmet."

"Is there some reason for that?" I said, watching the steam begin to rise from the coffee maker. "I mean, everybody likes good food, right?"

"They shoved those tasteless liquids down my throat for so long in the mental hospital that the truth is I don't even remember what 'good' means. But when I do eat something that everybody thinks is delicious, it's funny—I feel like something's draining out of me. Like something important is escaping from my body."

And what would that be?

"The mission I've been entrusted with. My destiny. Killing people."

When the noodles were ready, Frank handed me a plastic fork. I inhaled the fragrant steam, absorbing it like a sponge, then slurped up a mouthful before asking him if he was going to continue to kill people after hearing the hundred and eight bells. He shrugged.

"I never seemed to have much choice in the matter," he said. "Killing people has always been absolutely essential for me to go on living. Slashing my wrists and slicing through that swan's neck and drinking its blood and killing people were all basically expressions of the same thing, the thing that's driving me. If you don't keep your body and brain active, senility sets in, even if you're a little kid. The circulation in your brain gradually decreases. Like the cat in that experiment—by the time he lost interest in eating, the blood in his brain was just barely moving. It's the stress that does it. Human beings have thought up everything from hunting in groups to pop songs and car races so our brains wouldn't atrophy, but there aren't that many genuinely effective ways to guard against senility nowadays. Kids are especially vulnerable because their options are so limited. And now with all this social surveillance and manipulation going on, I think you'll see an increase in people like me."

Frank had speared some noodles with his fork and raised them to just below his chin but then seemed to forget about them as he rambled on. Condensation from his cup dripped onto the dusty floor. Eventually the steam ceased to rise from it, but he continued talking. He'd forgotten he was eating. Concentration wasn't the word for this—it was something much more intense, as if he were possessed. As if his life would end if he stopped talking. He hadn't taken a single bite of his ramen, and the stuff on the end of his fork had begun to change color. Listening to him talk on and on with one eye on the darkening noodles, I'd watched them transform into some unidentifiable, pendulous, stringy substance. When he paused in his monologue for a moment I raised my eyebrows at his fork and lifted my chin to suggest he eat. Glancing with some surprise at the noodles, he shoveled them in his mouth and chewed with a melancholy air that seemed to say: Why do we have to go through the dreary process of ingesting food?

"When I was twelve I killed three in a row—all old people sleeping on porches in their rocking chairs or gliders—and I made a tape taking credit for the murders and sent it to the local radio station. They had a DJ I liked and I wanted him to know I was the serial killer everyone was talking about. I did a lot of things to disguise my voice—packed cotton balls in my mouth, held a pencil between my teeth, scotch-taped my lips together, and so forth—and I used an old tape recorder of my father's. It took me over twenty hours to do it, but I can't tell you how much fun it was. In the end the FBI managed to analyze the voice print, which proved my guilt beyond any reasonable doubt, so for a long time I regretted making and sending that tape. But then years later I remembered what fun it had been, how it made me feel like I was getting in touch with things outside myself, like I finally fit properly into my own body. That's why I want to listen to those bells, Kenji: to see if my bad instincts—

my bonno—will be washed away, so I can fit into my own body again."

Moments after I finished my ramen, sleep began to steal over me. I rubbed my eyes, and Frank jerked his thumb at the mattress we were sitting on and told me I could sleep there. "It's not so easy to climb up to the second floor," he said. I lay down on the mattress in my suit and overcoat. Frank was still eating, and I put a hand over my eyes to block out the light from the lamp. He must have seen me do this, because he turned it off. The mattress was cold and damp. Sleep kept pulling me down, but the cold kept waking me back up. The warmth of the ramen I'd eaten was soon just a memory, and the cold seemed to seep up through the mattress from the floor. At some point I started shivering. I heard Frank rummaging around and then felt a crinkly sort of blanket being placed over me. When I moved, the blanket made a rustling sound, as if it was made of paper. Frank ate the rest of his ramen in total darkness. Just before I fell asleep I had a moment of panic, thinking he was going to kill me after all, but I reminded myself that he wouldn't do that before hearing the bells. As I drifted off, a bird was screeching somewhere outside.

I woke up covered with old newspapers. I heard Frank's voice say, "We won't be coming back here, so don't forget anything." I looked up to see him dressing. Improbably enough, he was climbing into a tuxedo. He said he'd been waiting for me to wake up.

"There are no mirrors here, so I need you to tell me if my tie is straight."

He wore trousers with a stripe running down the outside of each leg and was squirming into a shirt of some shiny material with lacy frills down the front. A bow tie and jacket were draped over the stack of cardboard boxes. "Pretty snazzy," I said, and he smiled as he buttoned the shirt. Watching Frank don a tuxedo in the dim light of this ruined building, with shards of broken glass scattered across the floor, I had to wonder if I wasn't still dreaming. I asked him if he'd brought the tux with him.

"Yeah, I did. Tuxedos are great when there's a celebration of some kind and you want to blend in."

It was only 4:00 P.M. when we left the building. I didn't know how big a crowd would show up at Kachidoki Bridge, and I wanted to be sure of grabbing the spot I told Jun we'd be at.

As Frank led the way down the narrow alley, I asked him if he'd been staying in that building since he came to Japan. He'd stayed at a hotel for a while but didn't feel comfortable there, he said. It had been so dark the night before that I hadn't noticed, but signs were posted all along the cul-de-sac: DANGER! TOXIC WASTE! KEEP OUT! When I stopped to read the first one we came to, Frank said something about "polychlorinated biphenyl."

"There used to be a factory here that made copy paper treated with PCB, and a wholesale distributor or two, and then when it was discovered that PCB is bad for you the authorities sealed off this whole area. Fact is, the toxic material, the dioxin, isn't released into the atmosphere unless the PCB is burned, but the cops don't know that and steer clear of the neighborhood. You couldn't ask for a better hideout."

He said he'd been told all this by a homeless man who spoke English with a British accent. The homeless man they found burned to a crisp? I didn't ask.

Frank wore a red muffler over his tuxedo and was carrying a small duffel bag. It was true, though, that he didn't stand out, even as we neared Yoyogi Station. I guess people just assumed we were on our way to a New Year's Eve party.

I led Frank to a soba shop in front of the station, explaining that on New Year's Eve it's customary to eat buckwheat noodles. I was starving. I asked for herring-and-soba soup and Frank ordered *zaru soba*—plain cold noodles. Several groups of college students were clustered around tables, eating and talking quietly, but none of them paid any attention to us. I didn't need to know much about clothes and fashion to see that Frank's tuxedo was a cheap one or that his muffler was a long way from cashmere. My own suit was wrinkled and dusty and didn't look as if it hadn't been slept in. Anyone observing a bit more closely might have thought us a suspicious pair, but the students completely ignored us, and I began to understand how Frank had managed such spectacular murders without getting caught. Right now in this country nobody gives a damn about strangers. I wondered if that was true in America too, and asked Frank about it while we waited for the food to come. He said it was true in the cities, at least.

The restaurant had no forks, and the chopsticks did nothing to speed up Frank's eating technique. It took him nearly an hour to finish his soba, by which time the noodles were dry and swollen and night had fallen outside. The kitchen was bustling as the small staff prepared for the crush of customers who'd show up just before midnight to greet the new year slurping up soba for good luck. The owner was a tiny old man who, when I apologized for taking so long, laughed and said: "Gaijin will be gaijin." It was an odd sensation to be sitting there with Frank and yet be treated like any other customer in a place as ordinary as a noodle shop outside a station. I was back in the everyday world, which only made the massacre of the night before all the more unreal to me. But part of me couldn't forget the very real horror of ears lopped off and throats slashed open. It was as though a thin membrane were covering only Frank and me, or as if we'd fallen deep inside some weird sort of fissure in the reality around us.

While Frank ate his soba I pored over every inch of an evening paper someone had left behind. There was no mention of the omiai pub. I was relieved but not surprised. Anyone who found the shutter down would simply assume the place had closed for the holidays. And even if the manager, for example, had a family, they'd probably hesitate to contact the police just because he went missing for a night or two, given the nature of his work. The bodies might not be discovered for days. How long does it take for a corpse to begin decomposing? Would the cold December temperatures slow the process?

Frank stabbed a clump of soba with his chopsticks and asked why we ate this stuff on New Year's Eve. I explained how the long buckwheat noodles symbolized hope for a long life. Gripping the chopsticks like a knife, he'd been sliding them under the strands and then trying to finesse them to his mouth. At first, when the noodles were still fresh and slippery, they'd tended to slip off as soon as he tried to lift them, but as they grew soft and swollen they clung to the sticks and made it easier, if less appetizing. Anyone who knew nothing about Frank would probably have been charmed or amused by his clumsy efforts to grapple with soba. I wasn't charmed, of course, but I wasn't amused either.

"What made the old-time Japanese think they wouldn't die if they ate soba?" Frank was taking this very seriously.

They didn't think they wouldn't die, I said, they thought they'd live longer. Frank shrugged and shook his head, and I realized he had a point. Living longer was the same as not dying, at least anytime soon. Maybe in this country "long life" meant something different from "postponed death." In any case, few Japanese would ever have considered the possibility of an outsider like Frank suddenly coming along and rubbing them out.

He was now sawing with his chopsticks at the dry, gray clump of buckwheat dough.

We rode the Yamanote Line to Yotsuya, descended to the subway, and transferred again at Ginza. Ginza Station was insanely crowded, and Frank didn't look happy as we waddled along with the herd. When I asked him if he disliked crowds, he said he was afraid of them.

"A lot of people jammed into one place really scares me, it always has. Which is not to say I like being all alone either. I just don't seem to have a stable comfort zone when it comes to personal space."

It was still early in the evening when we emerged onto a street in Tsukiji, near the fish market. From the top of a pedestrian overpass we caught a glimpse of Hongan-ji Temple. Frank said it looked like an Islamic mosque. He had left his duffel bag in a station coin locker after removing a gray raincoat, which he was now wearing. It was a plain one like the British often wear, and made him even less conspicuous. The road leading to Kachidoki Bridge was wide but dimly lit, with few shops or restaurants and only the occasional passing car. I'd never been here before. This was a very different Tokyo from places like Shibuya or Shinjuku. Wooden bait-and-tackle shops with disintegrating roofs and broken signs stood next to shiny new convenience stores, and futuristic highrise apartment complexes rose skyward on either side of narrow, retro streets lined with wholesalers of dried fish.

A gently arching old structure of steel and stone came into view. What a pretty bridge, Frank said softly. To the left of it, along the riverbank, stretched a narrow public park called Sumida River Terrace. Near the entrance to the park was a big rectangular stone basin with a fountain, but whether because of the season or because of the hour the water had been turned off. The New Year's bells wouldn't begin for quite some time yet, so we walked down through the park to the riverside and sat on a bench, where we had a good view of the bridge railing. This would be the perfect place for Jun to sit, I thought. Spaced every few meters along the bridge were metal lanterns, and reflections from the yellow lights wavered on the dark surface of the river. After the white fluorescent lights of the ruined clinic, the soba shop, and the trains, those lanterns felt like long-lost friends to me. A group of men who looked like migrant laborers from distant provinces sat drinking in a circle at the water's edge, not far from us. At first they'd been roasting something over a small fire, but then two policemen strolled over and asked them to put it out. The men did so without protest. Though night had long since fallen, flocks of pigeons whirled overhead from time to time. The white things I could see bobbing on the river were probably seagulls. I told Frank we still had a long wait before the bells began to sound. He adjusted his bow tie and said he was used to waiting.

The night wore on, but barely a breeze blew over the river, and it was much warmer than the past two nights had been. Frank was observing the interaction between the policemen and the circle of half-drunk laborers. The cops had made them douse the fire but weren't throwing their weight around. Once the fire was extinguished, they both sat down with the men and started chatting: Which part of the country are you from? Aren't you going home for New Year's? And so on. Apparently the men were all from the same region up north. They said they'd been unable to book train tickets for today so planned to spend the night here and head home tomorrow.

A crowd was gradually gathering in the park and on the bridge. Mostly young people in couples and groups. Some of the couples were drinking thermos cups of coffee and sharing sandwiches, others stood shoulder to shoulder listening to music on the same Walkman. One group was waving to each boat that passed. I figured they'd all read about this place in the same magazine Jun and I had seen. There was no sign of her yet.

The policemen walked toward me and Frank. No one else knew about the bodies in the omiai pub, so I was sure we weren't in danger of being arrested, but it didn't do my nerves any good to see two uniformed officers approaching, each with a long hardwood riot stick. There was no change whatsoever in Frank's expression.

"Komban wa," the older of the two said to us.

I returned the greeting—"Good evening"—and Frank, seated beside me, bobbed his head in an attempt at a bow. It was an endearingly clumsy gesture that said: Though an outsider here, I respect your culture and traditions. *"Gaijin-san desu ne. Joya-no-kane desu ka?"* asked the policeman, and I said: *"So desu."* Yes, he's a foreigner and we're here for the New Year's bells.

The policeman said he didn't think there'd be a very big crowd tonight, but we should nonetheless be on guard against pickpockets and bag-snatchers and what have you. I translated this for Frank, who bobbed his head again and said: *"Arigato gozaimasu."* The two policemen walked away smiling. "What friendly cops," Frank muttered as he watched them go.

More people were arriving, so we decided to walk over and claim our spot.

A homeless man was sitting on sheets of cardboard at the foot of the bridge, his belongings in a baby carriage. A foul smell radiated out from him. We gave him a wide berth and went up to lean against the railing, looking out over the river and the little park, to wait for the bells.

"I wonder which of us is more of a bane on society, that homeless fellow or me?" said Frank.

I asked him if he really thought single individuals could be "a bane on society."

"Of course they can," Frank said, his eyes still on the bum, "and I'm clearly more of one than he is. I see myself as being like a virus. Did you know that only a tiny minority of viruses cause illness in humans? No one knows how many viruses there are, but their real role, when you get right down to it, is to aid in mutations, to create diversity among life forms. I've read a lot of books on the subject—when you don't need much sleep you have a lot of time to read—and I can tell you that if it weren't for viruses, mankind would never have evolved on this planet. Some viruses get right inside the DNA and change your genetic code, did you know that? And no one can say for sure that HIV, for example, won't one day prove to have been rewriting our genetic code in a way that's essential to our survival as a race. I'm a man who consciously commits murders and scares the hell out of people and makes them reconsider everything, so I'm definitely malignant, yet I think I play a necessary role in this world. But people like him?"

Frank looked over at the homeless guy, who hadn't budged from his cardboard mat. On the bridge, the crowd continued to grow, but he alone had plenty of room.

"It's not that people like him have given up on life," Frank went on. "They've given up trying to relate to others. In poor countries you may have refugees but you don't have bums. The homeless in our societies have the easiest lives of anybody, in a way. If you reject society, then you should live outside it, not off it—you have to take some risks. I've done at least that much in my life. But people like him, they're not even capable of a life of crime.

They're examples of retrogression—devolution, I call it—and I've spent my life exterminating them."

Frank was speaking very slowly and clearly to make sure I followed him. He could be strangely persuasive when he talked like this, but part of me wasn't buying it. I wanted to ask him if the dismembered high-school girl was an example of devolution too, but I didn't have the energy.

Frank turned toward Sumida River Terrace and sent a jolt through me by saying: "There she is." Jun had materialized on a bench in the park. She glanced up at us, then quickly averted her eyes, bowing her head and staring at her feet, probably wondering what the hell to do now. I felt a sudden tidal wave of remorse for having summoned her to watch out for me. Not because Frank knew who she was, though I should have foreseen as much. After all, he'd found his way to my apartment and stuck a piece of charred human flesh to my door—how hard could it have been for him to get a good look at Jun's face? But I never should have asked an innocent creature like her to come anywhere near this monster. Looking at Jun I saw the world Before Frank, and the huge gulf between her and the post-Frank me. I should have dealt with this on my own, whatever the cost. I shouldn't have got her involved, I thought, and looked around for a policeman. *I have to protect Jun*: the moment this thought crystallized in my mind, my feelings disengaged completely from Frank. It was like being released from a spell. I even realized what it was about Frank's argument that I couldn't swallow. Who was he to set himself up as judge and jury? No one could possibly tell who is or isn't an example of devolution, even if there was such a thing.

"I can tell, Kenji." My heart froze. "Sometimes I know what people are thinking. Not all the time, mind you. If it happened all the time I'd go insane. But when you're killing, your senses have to be wide open and honed to razor sharpness. You have to be totally *there*. When I kill, I get so focused that I can pick up certain signals people send out, unconscious signals that emanate from the blood circulating in their brains. Sluggish brain circulation is one of the hallmarks of devolution, and it causes a signal that says: PLEASE KILL ME.

Kenji, you're the only friend I've made in Japan—in fact you may be the only real friend I've ever had. Go on now, go to your girlfriend. Thank you for bringing me here. I won't impose on you any longer. I'll go off someplace where I can listen to the bells on my own."

Frank jerked his chin toward Jun, dismissing me. But when I turned in a daze to walk away, he clamped his hand on my shoulder. "I almost forgot to give you this," he said, and held out an envelope. "It's a present. Something very valuable to me, much more valuable than any amount of money, and I want you to have it."

As I took the envelope, he added: "There's just one thing I was hoping we could do that we never got around to. I wanted to have some miso soup with you, but it's too late now. We won't be meeting again."

"Miso soup?"

"Yeah. I'm really interested in miso soup. I ordered it at a little sushi bar in Colorado once long ago, and I thought it was a darned peculiar kind of soup, the smell it had and everything, so I didn't eat it, but it intrigued me. It had that funny brown color and smelled kind of like human sweat, but it also looked delicate and refined somehow. I came to this country hoping to find out what the people who eat that soup on a daily basis might be like. So I'm a little disappointed we didn't get to have some together."

I asked him if he was going back to America right away. No, not right away, he said, so I suggested we could still have miso soup together sometime. Even the smallest Japanese restaurant has it, I explained, and you can even buy it in convenience stores. That's all right, Frank said with a smile—that peculiar smile of his which looked as if his features weren't relaxing but collapsing.

"I don't need to eat the stuff now because now I'm here—right in the middle of it! The soup I ordered in Colorado had all these little slices of vegetables and things, which at the time just looked like kitchen scrapings to me. But now I'm in the miso soup myself, just like those bits of vegetable. I'm floating around in this giant bowl of it, and that's good enough for me."

Frank and I shook hands, and I turned and walked toward Jun's park bench. My entire body was rigid with tension. Jun looked puzzled as she glanced from me to Frank and back again. The New Year's bells still hadn't begun to sound. I was deviating from the script, and she didn't know what to do. She pointed at the bridge. I looked back and Frank was gone. Jun shook her head to tell me she didn't know where.

I opened the envelope beneath a streetlamp. It was sealed with seven of the little Print Club photo stickers of Frank and me. Me before I knew anything, standing there looking disgruntled, and Frank beside me with his poker face. Inside the envelope was a gray, soiled feather.

"What's that?" Jun asked, pressing against me.

"The feather of a swan," I said.

A NOTE ON THE AUTHOR

Renaissance man for the postmodern age, Ryu Murakami has played drums for a rock group, made movies and hosted a TV talk show. His first novel *Almost Transparent Blue*, written while he was still a student, was awarded Japan's most coveted literary prize and went on to sell over a million copies.

A NOTE ON THE TRANSLATOR

Ralph McCarthy is the translator of *69* by Ryu Murakami and two collections of stories by Osamu Dazzai.